GET A̶L̶L̶ ̶T̶H̶E̶S̶E̶

WITH JUST O̶N̶E̶

$50 VALUE

◆ **Hotel Discounts** up to 60% at home and abroad

◆ **Travel Service** - Guaranteed lowest published airfares plus 5% cash back on tickets ◆ **$25 Travel Voucher**

◆ **Sensuous Petite Parfumerie** collection ◆ **Insider Tips Letter** with sneak previews of upcoming books

You'll get a FREE personal card, too. It's your passport to all these benefits– and to even more great gifts & benefits to come!

There's no club to join. No purchase commitment. No obligation.

WL-PP6A

Enrollment Form

☐ **Yes!** I WANT TO BE A **PRIVILEGED WOMAN.**
Enclosed is one *PAGES & PRIVILEGES*™ Proof of
Purchase from any Harlequin or Silhouette book currently for
sale in stores (Proofs of Purchase are found on the back pages
of books) and the store cash register receipt. Please enroll me
in *PAGES & PRIVILEGES*™. Send my Welcome Kit and FREE
Gifts -- and activate my FREE benefits -- immediately.

More great gifts and benefits to come.

NAME (please print)

ADDRESS   APT. NO

CITY   STATE   ZIP/POSTAL CODE

PROOF OF PURCHASE ONLY

NO CLUB!
NO COMMITMENT!
*Just one purchase brings
you great Free Gifts and
Benefits!*

Please allow 6-8 weeks for delivery. Quantities are limited. We reserve the right to
substitute items. Enroll before October 31, 1995 and receive one full year of benefits.

Name of store where this book was purchased_____

Date of purchase_____

Type of store:
☐ Bookstore   ☐ Supermarket   ☐ Drugstore
☐ Dept. or discount store (e.g. K-Mart or Walmart)
☐ Other (specify)_____

Which Harlequin or Silhouette series do you usually read?

Complete and mail with one Proof of Purchase and store receipt to:
U.S.: *PAGES & PRIVILEGES*™, P.O. Box 1960, Danbury, CT 06813-1960
Canada: *PAGES & PRIVILEGES*™, 49-6A The Donway West, P.O. 813,
North York, ON M3C 2E8

WL-PP6B

▼ DETACH HERE AND MAIL TODAY! ▼

Hi.

My name is Kevin Cole and I'm six years old. Even though Aunt Kristi is my dad's sister, I know her husband, Uncle Jason, better 'cause he lives on the ranch next to ours and Aunt Kristi has been living in New York most of my life. 'Course, she sends me and my sister, Kari, cards and gifts and things, but she won't ever come to see us. I heard my dad say it's 'cause she's still hurtin' and doesn't want to face Uncle Jason. I don't know why she's hurtin', though. All I know is she's a real famous model with her picture on the front of magazines and in perfume ads and lots of places.

I like my uncle Jason a lot. He comes over and plays with me, and lets me ride horseback with him and my dad. Once I asked him why he didn't have children and he looked real sad and said that was a story for another time. I bet he'd make a good daddy, though.

It's hard to understand grown-ups sometimes. My mom tried to explain how people can love each other and still can't work out their problems, but that didn't make much sense to me. I mean, if you love someone, then don't you want to be around them all the time?

Maybe someday soon Aunt Kristi will come back and Uncle Jason will convince her not to ever leave him again.

I hope so. I'd sure like to have some cousins to play with.

KEVIN

Ranch Rogues
1. Betrayed by Love
   Diana Palmer
2. Blue Sage
   Anne Stuart
3. Chase the Clouds
   Lindsay McKenna
4. Mustang Man
   Lee Magner
5. Painted Sunsets
   Rebecca Flanders
6. Carved in Stone
   Kathleen Eagle

Hitched in Haste
7. A Marriage of Convenience
   Doreen Owens Malek
8. Where Angels Fear
   Ginna Gray
9. Mountain Man
   Joyce Thies
10. The Hawk and the Honey
    Dixie Browning
11. Wild Horse Canyon
    Elizabeth August
12. Someone Waiting
    Joan Hohl

Ranchin' Dads
13. Ramblin' Man
    Barbara Kaye
14. His and Hers
    Pamela Bauer
15. The Best Things in Life
    Rita Clay Estrada
16. All That Matters
    Judith Duncan
17. One Man's Folly
    Cathy Gillen Thacker
18. Sagebrush and Sunshine
    Margot Dalton

Denim & Diamonds
19. Moonbeams Aplenty
    Mary Lynn Baxter
20. In a Class by Himself
    JoAnn Ross
21. The Fairy Tale Girl
    Ann Major
22. Snow Bird
    Lass Small
23. Soul of the West
    Suzanne Ellison
24. Heart of Ice
    Diana Palmer

Kids & Kin
25. Fools Rush In
    Ginna Gray
26. Wellspring
    Curtiss Ann Matlock
27. Hunter's Prey
    Annette Broadrick
28. Laughter in the Rain
    Shirley Larson
29. A Distant Promise
    Debbie Bedford
30. Family Affair
    Cathy Gillen Thacker

Reunited Hearts
31. Yesterday's Lies
    Lisa Jackson
32. Tracings on a Window
    Georgia Bockoven
33. Wild Lady
    Ann Major
34. Cody Daniels' Return
    Marilyn Pappano
35. All Things Considered
    Debbie Macomber
36. Return to Yesterday
    Annette Broadrick

Reckless Renegades
37. Ambushed
    Patricia Rosemoor
38. West of the Sun
    Lynn Erickson
39. A Wild Wind
    Evelyn A. Crowe
40. The Deadly Breed
    Caroline Burnes
41. Desperado
    Helen Conrad
42. Heart of the Eagle
    Lindsay McKenna

Once A Cowboy...
43. Rancho Diablo
    Anne Stuart
44. Big Sky Country
    Jackie Merritt
45. A Family to Cherish
    Cathy Gillen Thacker
46. Texas Wildcat
    Lindsay McKenna
47. Not Part of the Bargain
    Susan Fox
48. Destiny's Child
    Ann Major

Please address questions and book requests to: Silhouette Reader Service
U.S.: 3010 Walden Ave., P.O. Box 1325, Buffalo, NY 14269
Canadian: P.O. Box 609, Fort Erie, Ont. L2A 5X3

KIDS 'N KIN

WESTERN *Lovers*

ANNETTE BROADRICK

HUNTER'S PREY

Silhouette Books

Published by Silhouette Books

America's Publisher of Contemporary Romance

To Pinkie,
with love…

SILHOUETTE BOOKS
300 East 42nd St.,
New York, N.Y. 10017

ISBN 0-373-88527-X

HUNTER'S PREY

One

She saw him cross the hotel lobby, his boots clicking a staccato rhythm on the marble surface. From her vantage point near the dining area, she watched when he paused at the cave-like entrance to the lounge, removing his Stetson as he surveyed the room. Only after he had disappeared into the gloom did Kristine Cole discover she'd forgotten to breathe when she saw him. Jason McAlister had always had that effect on her.

His appearance miles from where she expected to find him temporarily banished all

thoughts of food from her mind. With a start
Kristi registered the weary patience on the
hostess's face as she waited to show her to her
table. Kristi smiled her apology and followed
the elegant woman to a small table tucked between potted palms.

The hotel was Holiday Inn's contribution
toward the growth of the small southwest
Texas town near where Kristi grew up. It was
built at the cloverleaf of the interstate highway that skirted Cielo, and neither the highway nor the hotel had been there when she left
Texas five years before.

Jason McAlister was the reason she had not
returned sooner. He was also responsible for
her being there now.

What should I do? she wondered, chewing
on her bottom lip. She'd driven her Triumph
TR7 from New York, taking her time, enjoying the freedom of being on her own after
years of restrictive schedules and demanding
deadlines. She had stopped at the hotel on im-
pulse. A night's rest before driving the final
fifty miles to her brother's ranch had seemed
like a good idea earlier in the evening. Now she
wasn't so sure.

Of course, Kristi intended to contact Jason—she just hadn't counted on seeing him quite so soon. Why should she be nervous? She'd mingled with the rich and royalty, politicians and playboys. Why should one particular rancher in an obscure part of Texas cause butterflies to flutter up under her ribs? Why indeed?

What should I do? she asked herself once more. The dignified waiter standing with pencil poised implied that she could order her dinner as far as he was concerned.

Good idea. Without glancing at the menu, she said, "The dinner salad, please." His blank face almost registered an expression of surprise as his eyes scanned her slender figure.

Of course I'm thin, she thought with irritation. *That's because models go around half-starved most of the time.* She gave him her dazzling smile as an apology for her waspish thoughts.

"Will there be anything else?"

"A glass of chablis, please." *Hang the calories, I need a drink.* Her insides continued to quiver like jelly in an earthquake. Of course she didn't *have* to face him tonight. She could stick with her original plan to visit with Kyle and Francine for a few days, then call Jason and arrange to meet with him.

The waiter returned with her drink and it was only when she caught sight of her trembling hand as she reached for the glass that Kristi faced how unnerved she was. Lifting the glass to her lips, she managed to spill a drop or two on her muted green ultrasuede dress. She ineffectually dabbed at the spots with her napkin, her appearance the least of her concerns at that moment.

No one in her family could explain the genetic accident that gave Kristi her striking good looks. High cheekbones created mysterious shadows, and slanted eyes tantalized with the glitter of emeralds. Rioting waves of fiery hair held a shimmering life all their own, and when photographers discovered how her translucent skin glowed under their powerful lamps, her career was off and running. Her face now gazed from countless magazine covers in the States as well as in western Europe.

Kristi Cole was a celebrity but not in southwest Texas.

Would Jason find her changed? She bore scant resemblance to the teenaged tomboy who preferred Levi's and horses to satin and symphonies. However, inside she was the same person who'd spent her life in love with Jason McAlister.

Jason hadn't changed—physically at least. He still reminded Kristi of the mountain lion she once saw years ago while exploring the sand caves along the Rio Grande with Jason and her brother, Kyle. He moved with the same lazy grace, muscles rippling below the skin. Even his coloring was similar, his tawny hair sunstreaked a lighter shade than his skin, which was bronzed by the sun.

Kristi finished her salad. There was no reason to delay their meeting. He'd ignored her letters and refused to discuss the details of the divorce with her attorney, so she'd returned to Texas to face him.

Five years was long enough to overcome her feelings of loss and inadequacy. She had failed as his wife, but had become a success in her chosen career. She'd come to terms with the past, but needed to cut all ties to be entirely free.

With her chin slightly elevated, Kristi crossed the lobby to the darkened lounge. Following Jason's earlier example, she paused in the archway, her eyes adjusting to the lack

of light. Candle-filled globes formed oases of
light in the darkened room, silhouetting the
occupants of the lounge. Cigarette smoke lent
a mauve haze to the atmosphere. Near the
door well-cushioned barstools held a half
dozen men, and every man's eyes focused on
Kristi as she stood there searching the room.

She was used to receiving stares and ignored
them. The bartender paused in the midst of
drying a glass and stared as though trying to
place her. One of the men on the closest bar-
stool smiled as Kristi hovered in the doorway.

"Lose somebody, honey? Or are you just
looking for some company?"

A flash of green fire took in the man sitting
there, his flabby stomach hanging over a polished silver belt buckle, his blue-and-white
checked western shirt straining at the snaps.
Her face composed, Kristi gazed at him without speaking until his smile faltered and his
eyes dropped. She returned her attention to the
room and took a graceful step forward. A
slight turn of a tawny head in the back of the
lounge caught the candlelight and glinted gold.

He was still there—alone.

Jason sipped his bourbon and water and
watched the tall, slender woman make her

cautious way through the crowded room. His jaw tightened. One of the soft lights briefly highlighted the red of the woman's hair and a familiar pain throbbed inside him. Why did every tall, redheaded woman he saw remind him of Kristi?

As she moved closer he studied her with cynical regard. Someone out looking for companionship. He certainly wasn't in the mood to provide it. When Alvarez called to arrange a meeting Jason had almost put him off, despite his urgent need to get the information Alvarez supposedly had for him. The call from Kristi's lawyer had been all he wanted to handle in one day.

How many times did he have to say it? He didn't want a divorce. He'd finally learned to live with the knowledge that Kristi preferred a career in New York to living with him. He'd finally given up hoping that she'd eventually return home. He shook his head and took another sip. He'd learned to live with the constant loneliness and the pain of knowing he'd been unable to offer what she wanted from life. There was no way he'd ever be able to give her up completely. She was too much a part of him.

Kristi moved toward Jason. As she approached him, Jason raised his head, glancing at her from below heavy brows. His topaz eyes took in the length of her and, without meeting her eyes for more than an instant, his gaze dropped to his glass once again.

Kristi paused, shocked at the icy glare from Jason. He didn't recognize her. Even though she was aware of the drastic changes in her appearance, his cold expression had caught her off guard. She sank into an empty leather bench seat at the table next to his, her knees refusing to support her any longer.

Her mind whirled with bewilderment. After she had steeled herself for a confrontation, he hadn't even recognized her! She peered around the dimly lit room. Perhaps she might have had the same problem if she had not seen him earlier in the clear light of the lobby.

Now she faced the dilemma of whether to tell him who she was or to pretend she didn't know him. There was no reason for her not to stay and have a drink—she didn't have to speak to him. Tension eased from her at the thought.

From beneath thick lashes her eyes surreptitiously sought him as he sat there studying his drink, a bottle of bourbon near his elbow. Here was one change in his lifestyle—the Jason she remembered had an occasional cold beer on a hot day, no more.

A blond waitress paused at her table, her shapely legs revealed in fishnet stockings under a micro-mini black skirt. "What would you like?" She gave Kristi a haughty stare.

"A glass of chablis, please."

The woman flounced away. Kristi knew her thoughts as though they'd been spoken out loud. No one from around here drank wine—that was for Yankees and foreigners.

Kristi glanced up and caught Jason staring at her. Her heart leaped and began to pound in her chest like a herd of galloping horses.

Her voice had caught his attention. He hadn't talked to Kristi in years. He'd refused to torture himself by calling and listening to her soft voicc. The woman at the next table had the same husky contralto, but there was no trace of a southern speech pattern in her words. Her voice was crisp and controlled. The flickering light cast shadows over her as his eyes settled on her hands, which were resting lightly on the table, the frosted pink polish on her nails glinting in the candlelight.

Kristi could feel Jason's gaze as he studied her. Her hard-earned poise helped her to stay composed. She refused to glance at him, determined to have her drink and leave.

"Would you like to dance, little lady?"

Kristi glanced up, startled. Silver belt buckle from the bar had decided to make his move. She gave him a polite smile. "No, thank you."

"Aw, c'mon, lady. No reason not to be friendly, is there?" His Coors courage seemed to convince him she could only find him irresistible.

"The lady said no, Herman. Just leave it." The sound of Jason's voice shot through Kristi as though she had touched a hot-wired fence. He stood there by her table, facing hefty Herman with a level stare.

"I didn't mean nothin', Mac, you know that," Herman muttered.

"Sure, I know that, but this young lady doesn't know you as well as I do." He watched Herman as he made his embarrassed way back to the bar, to the catcalls and comments of his drinking buddies.

Kristi gave Jason a tentative smile. "Thank you."

He stood there, an intent expression on his face. "At the risk of sounding like another Herman, would you mind if I joined you? I never did care to drink alone."

His lazy smile caused a problem with her breathing. *I can't sit here with him and not tell him who I am*, she thought with dismay.

Bemused, she nodded her head. He reached back and gathered his bottle, glass and money from the other table, then slid onto the bench across from her. Her uncertain gaze fell on his hands. A shiver ran through her at the memories evoked by those sensitive fingers. She noticed the wedding band with a pang.

Kristi was intrigued with the idea of meeting Jason as an equal after all these years. The ten-year difference in their ages had caused the eighteen-year-old Kristi to feel at a disadvantage during most of the months they'd lived together after their marriage. She took a deep breath and forced herself to relax. How long dared she continue the pretense?

"You don't live around here," he said before she had a chance to speak. The comment was more of a statement than a question.

"That's right. I'm just visiting."

Her voice kept striking chords within him. How could two women have the same voice, or similar enough to cause such a gut-wrenching reaction within him?

The waitress brought her drink but, before Kristi could remove the money from her clutch purse, Jason pulled a couple of singles from the stack of bills lying beside his glass. He shoved them toward the waitress. Kristi dipped her head in mute thanks, raised her glass in a brief toast, then sipped from the tulip-shaped goblet.

"Do you come here often?" she asked, her head slightly tilted.

He looked at her with surprise. "Once in a while. Why?"

She smiled as she tipped her head toward the blond waitress who watched them covertly as she cleared a table nearby. "The barmaid has a rather possessive air where you're concerned."

He shrugged his unconcern. "Most everybody around here knows everybody else." He picked up his glass, drank half of its contents, then set it down.

Kristi studied the face before her. Sunlines fanned from his eyes, and the curves around his mouth had deepened. Strands of streaked gold fell across his forehead and teased Kristi's memory. She wanted to touch his face, to brush the hair from his forehead.

"Where're you from?" he asked, his tone polite. His eyes glowed in the soft light, the look of interest ensnaring Kristi as effectively as a rope. She wondered suspiciously if he were playing some kind of game with her.

"New York." Surely he'd respond to that information. How many tall redheads from New York showed up in Cielo these days, anyway?

In the same polite tone, he inquired, "What're you doing out here?"

Now was the time to tell him. I'm here to see you, Jason. We need to agree to the terms that will dissolve our relationship. Instead, she heard herself say, "I'm on vacation, so I thought I'd come out this way." *The truth as far as it went,* she thought, dismayed by her cowardice.

"Are you trying to interview the natives or something? See how we survive in our primitive conditions out West?" His grin took away any sting in the words. He finished the contents of his glass and poured another, then reached into his pocket for a cigarette. He offered her one, and when she gave him a quick shake of her head, bent his head to the burning match and touched his cigarette to the flame.

The blonde materialized by his shoulder. "Jay-son," she drawled, making his name into two words. "There's a Mr. Alvarez on the phone. Says he wants to talk to you."

Jason looked startled at the interruption, glancing at his watch in surprise. Excusing himself, he moved away from the table with catlike strides.

She remembered once accusing him of having Indian blood because of the silent way he moved. He'd laughed and ruffled her carrot-colored curls and admitted that most families who had spent years on the western plains of Texas had some Indian blood. The families never discussed it and certain strong features were ignored. Excited at the thought of such a romantic notion, Kristi had raced home to ask Kyle if they could have Indian blood as well. She still remembered his laughing at her gullibility.

Jason would not be amused when he discovered who she was. Then again, what if he already knew but was trying to figure out what she was hoping to accomplish by pretending not to know him? She herself wasn't sure.

If only she weren't so intrigued by the lazy masculinity that emanated from him. Her pulse rate hadn't slowed since she walked into the lounge. At this rate, Jason's presence would be as good for her as an hour of aerobics.

Kristi felt his anger when Jason returned to the table. He signaled the blonde to bring Kristi another drink, then poured himself one from the bottle, adding water.

"Is something wrong?" She'd always respected Jason's ability to control his emotions, almost envying him the skill at times, but it was obvious he was battling for that control at the moment.

"The man I was supposed to meet tonight can't make it. He left it a little late telling me." His drawl sounded more pronounced. He moved his hand until it rested against hers. "Care to dance?"

His question surprised her. She'd just about decided to leave. Kristi couldn't handle watching Jason drink so much.

He saw her surprise at his question. Actually, it surprised him as well. He wasn't interested in the woman except for her haunting resemblance to Kristi. Funny this woman should be from New York, too. Not that it mattered, he'd never see her again after tonight. So what was wrong with a dance? He'd like to forget Kristi, forget Alvarez, and forget the feeling of helplessness that threatened to engulf him.

Kristi rose from the table and started toward the center of the room. Two other couples swayed on the postage-stamp dance floor to the slow melody of Kenny Rogers's latest hit. She turned, ready for him to take her hand. Instead, Jason pulled her close against him, wrapping both arms around her. Kristi had no option but to place her hands on his shoulders. She felt the heavy muscles there flex as her hands slid around his neck. The years melted away as she caught the scent of his after-shave. The spicy fragrance teased at her as it evoked vivid memories. This man had always had a shattering effect on her.

When she'd left him, Kristi had buried her emotions deep inside herself. As time passed she eventually heard the name given to her by disgruntled males: the ice princess. It never bothered her because it was true. She didn't want to be touched. Yet as soon as Jason's arms slipped around her the ice began to melt. She relaxed against him.

The woman in his arms was too thin for his taste. His hands could almost reach around her tiny waist. When was the last time he'd danced? He couldn't remember, exactly. He'd taken Kristi somewhere.... Jason relaxed as the memories flowed around him. She'd always felt so good in his arms, whether they'd been on the dance floor or in bed. It was unfortunate this woman was so near the same height. He didn't need any more reminders. Not tonight.

Jason was light on his feet. He moved to the slow rhythm of the love song, his hands unconsciously caressing Kristi's back. They stayed on the dance floor until the musicians took a break, then returned to their table in silence.

Kristi took a large swallow of wine, almost choking. Her head spun from the intoxication of Jason's body pressed so intimately against her. Is this how he spends his time these days, she wondered? The sharp pain that shot through her at the thought shocked her with its intensity. Why should it matter to her? She'd made her decision months ago. They had no future together. She'd always wondered why he hadn't ended their marriage—he'd never made a secret of his dream of a large family. The familiar nagging sense of inadequacy niggled at the edges of her mind.

She'd had enough. Jason didn't recognize her or he would have said something by now. She looked at the bottle sitting there and shook her head slightly. Her memories had betrayed her. This man? This man wasn't the one she'd married. Her Jason would never have gone to a bar to drink and flirt with anyone who came in.

Kristi gave him a polite smile. "Thank you for the dance—and the drinks." She slid along the bench seat. "I think I'll go on to bed now—it's been a long day." As she started to get up, Jason pulled a cigarette from his mouth without lighting it, his eyes flicking over her with amused contempt.

"Is that an invitation?"

It took a moment for the sarcasm and sudden change of mood to penetrate Kristi's consciousness. She flushed a fiery red at the insult.

"I beg your pardon?" If the glittering green ice from her eyes hadn't warned him, the glacial tone of voice should have told Jason he'd made a serious mistake. He missed both.

"Maybe they do things differently in New York, but here in Texas a man likes to do his own running."

Grabbing her purse, Kristi rose with a smoothness that belied the tumult of rage threatening to overcome her. In a low, cool voice she let him have it. "Why, you supercilious, egotistical, drunken excuse for a west Texas cowboy, if I were looking for a companion, I could do a lot better than you!"

She spun on her heel and left through the outside door of the lounge. As soon as the door whispered closed behind her, Kristi stood on the walkway and took deep breaths, consciously calming her temper, glad to be away from the smoke and the smell of stale liquor.

Oh, how she wished she hadn't seen him tonight! She would have preferred her memories to the reality. The man she'd left just now bore little resemblance to the Jason McAlister she'd loved and married six years ago. Her decision to divorce him never seemed more right to her.

She followed the sidewalk as it wound its way through a miniature garden on the grounds of the large complex. Her fire-engine red Triumph sat in front of her motel door. She paused, fumbling in her bag for the room key, then inserted it into the door.

She turned the knob and started to push when a large hand reached past her and shoved on the door. Another hand gently propelled her through the opening.

Kristi gasped and spun around, then almost reeled with surprise. Jason stood there waiting for her reaction. Once again his silent approach had not warned her of his presence. Only now she was no longer impressed with his talent.

Her jaw hardened. "Get out of my room."

He glanced around, taking in the open suitcase at the end of the king-size bed, the few feminine items lying on the dresser and the sheer nightgown casually tossed across the pillows. The bright little car he'd seen outside was in keeping with her image of casual elegance.

Jason moved to the door, shut it, then turned to face her. He shoved his hat off his forehead and leaned lazily against the door. Kristi had left only the dressing area light on when she'd gone for dinner, and they stood in dusky shadows as they faced each other.

Jason pulled himself away from the door and approached Kristi, who stood by the bed. "I owe you an apology. I shouldn't have jumped to conclusions back there." He stopped when he came within arm's length of her.

Kristi looked him over from the tip of his boots to the top of his Stetson, then flicked her gaze to meet his. With something close to contempt, she said, "You made a mistake, cowboy, but so did I. It was just a case of mistaken identity." She kept her chin high and her gaze steady.

He placed both of his hands around the curve of her neck in a gentle, caressing movement. His thumbs rested on each side of her jaw and massaged the area as he studied her face. "Funny you should say that, because I've been feeling the same thing about you, Miss New York. What's your name?"

She knew he must feel the pounding of her pulse beneath his hands, a pounding that had started as soon as he touched her. Her breath fluttered in her throat like a trapped bird trying to fly free. She was surprised to hear her voice sound so unaffected. "It doesn't matter."

All she wanted was for him to get out of her room. She would deal with the legal termination of their relationship tomorrow. Tonight she had a dream to bury.

"You're right," he muttered, "it doesn't matter." His mouth swooped down on hers. One arm moved behind her, effectively imprisoning her against his long, lean body, hard from years of physical labor. With his other hand he raked through her hair, which was pinned up, causing it to tumble down her back in a cascade of fiery flame.

His mouth surprised her with its soft, searching movement on hers. She'd expected a brutal assault that didn't materialize. Instead, his mouth caressed hers until his tongue began to outline the shape of her lips, coaxing its way through the barrier of her lips and teeth.

Damn him! How could he continue to have such an effect on her? She had thought she was over him; obviously, she wasn't. Her feelings for him were confused—but intense. She loved him—she hated him—she longed for him—she had to be free of him. But oh! It felt good to be in his arms again. Was it wrong to want to love him and hold him one last time? All of the locked-up feelings Kristi had carried for this man for so long were released.

With a groan she responded to his kiss. She wrapped her arms around his neck and ran her fingers through the golden strands that had tempted her earlier in the evening. She felt more than heard the muffled moan he made as her response registered.

Kristi felt the edge of the bed against the back of her legs. As she fell over, Jason followed her down without loosening his grip. His mouth continued to explore hers and his hands moved gently over her shoulders as though memorizing her. He found the hidden zipper at the V-neck of her dress and slid it down a few inches. His thigh moved between hers, pushing her skirt into folds around her hips, and his body pressed against her. He emphasized his possession as his mouth slipped from hers to explore her neck and the hollow between her breasts. He moved the zipper down until the lace from her bikini briefs was her only protection from his exploring hands.

A tremor shook her when his mouth eased over her breast. She reached for the buttons on his shirt and began unsnapping them, then tugged the shirt from his chest so she could feel his bare skin against hers.

He shuddered as he felt her warm flesh caress his. Her dress was in the way, and Jason slid it from her while he explored her body with work-roughened hands. She had never forgotten the touch of those hands as they taught her the intricacies of lovemaking.

He moved with controlled patience and subdued passion over her body, loving her with his mouth and hands. Her bones turned to liquid as his hand rubbed against her inner thigh, paused, then began a coaxing rhythm that caused her to quiver in response.

She was stunned when he moved away from her, slipping from the bed. He couldn't leave now! Her body ached for his possession. Then she realized that he was pulling off his boots and sliding out of the snug Levi's that clung to his muscular thighs. When he moved back to cover her with his body, she arched into him, wanting to feel his strength once more.

Kristi trembled as Jason's kisses slid down her breasts, then traced an invisible line to the top of her thighs. Only this man had the power to reduce her to a quivering mass of sensations. She needed him desperately. How had she ever survived without his tender strength and fierce passion?

The tension built within her and she moved her hips in an unconscious invitation as his hands readied her. He eased himself into her with a control that harnessed the powerful need building inside of him. She wrapped her legs around his hips in a possessive hold. For the moment, he belonged to her. For the moment, that was enough.

The stamina and endurance built up over years of long, grueling physical activity enabled Jason to take them both to the far reaches of the universe. Kristi felt the sudden release of her own body as it continued to cling to him, but he never slackened his rhythm and the driving force of his possession of her.

Time lost all meaning as they moved together in the choreographed moves of lovemaking, their bodies glistening with moisture. Jason's pace became more urgent and she heard his anguished cry as she felt him explode within her. At the same time her body responded once more with rapid contractions that drained him while fulfilling them both. As her arms convulsively squeezed him to her, he collapsed and his weight descended, holding her prisoner. "Oh, Jase," she murmured, as he slid to one side, his arms and legs clamped securely around her.

Kristi floated in the afterglow of their tempestuous coming together and descended only when she realized what he'd said in his hoarse cry. Her name had echoed on his lips. Had it been a game with him and he'd known who she was all along? She pulled away and discovered that he was sound asleep. The combination of the whiskey and the exertion of their lovemaking had knocked him out. Was he even aware of having spoken her name? She had no way of knowing.

As Kristi contemplated the sleeping face next to her, she wasn't at all sure she hadn't received a metaphorical slap in the face. However, even in his sleep he hadn't let her go. She tried to shift away from him and his arms tightened. She relaxed. It was obvious she wasn't going anywhere. After traveling many miles and several years, Kristi was right back where she started—in Jason's arms.

A brilliant shaft of sunlight pierced Jason's heavy sleep. He woke with a start and looked around the empty room in bewilderment.

What was he doing here? He peered at his watch and flinched at the time. It was after nine o'clock. He groaned.

He felt as though a hundred miniature soldiers were marching in his head, each of their tiny steps sending shooting pains through his brain, while his mouth felt as though someone had stuffed it full of dirty socks.

He had really done it this time. He should have been at the ranch hours ago with the day's assignments for the hands. Instead he had a thirty-five-mile drive to look forward to with the tiny soldiers marching on.

He knew better than to drink hard liquor. After a couple of drinks he saw Kristi everywhere. Getting that call from her lawyer hadn't helped, either, but he refused to excuse his behavior. After all these years without Kristi, he'd finally succumbed to the charms of another woman. She had had the same coloring and was the same height as Kristi, but otherwise she had borne little resemblance to the fun-loving, impetuous girl he remembered. Then again, maybe that Kristi existed only in his memories. He'd seen no sign of her in the cold letters requesting his cooperation in gaining her freedom which he'd been receiving from her these past several months.

There was no way in hell he was going to let her divorce him. If she thought differently, she was going to find herself with a Texas-size fight on her hands.

What had possessed him to follow the woman out of the bar? He vaguely remembered their conversation but couldn't recall what he'd said to make her jump up and leave. He must have followed her to apologize, but somehow he couldn't recollect why. Or how he came to spend the night. He had flashes of memory of her sleek body as he'd pulled her clothes away from her. She certainly hadn't put up a struggle!

Damn it! He wasn't some adolescent kid to be lured into a stranger's bed. He knew better than that! Jason pulled himself up and sat on the side of the bed, his painful head buried in his hands. "Serves you right, you stupid bastard," he muttered in disgust.

His pants lay in a crumpled heap beside the bed. Jason leaned over very carefully in case his head should decide to tumble off his shoulders. He managed to stand and pull the pants up to his narrow waist and fasten them.

Within five minutes he let himself out the door, his hat in his hand, his wrinkled shirt pulled hastily over his broad chest. As he turned he noticed that the little sports car was gone. That suited him just fine. He sincerely hoped he'd never see the lady again. As a matter of fact, he couldn't really remember what she looked like. He hoped she'd have the same problem.

His pickup sat in the parking lot where he'd left it. With economical movements he got in and drove off. He planned to stop at the first restaurant he spotted for some much-needed coffee and aspirin.

Damn Alvarez, anyway! I ordered the bourbon for him. Why didn't he show up? He knows we're fighting time on this deal.

His mind skipped back to a picture of warm flesh glowing in the dim light; saucy breasts with pink tips luring him to touch, to taste, and to enjoy. He shook his head, stirring the tiny soldiers once more, and groaned.

A half hour later he pulled into a truck stop and carefully crawled out of the cab of his pickup, determined to forget the night.

Two

The warm Texas sun felt good on Kristi's neck and shoulders as she turned onto the farm road leading to her brother's ranch. By the time she'd finished breakfast, it had been warm enough so that she could put the top down on her car.

It was mild for April. Spring was already putting touches of lime green to many of the trees, and wild flowers were beginning to peek through the tall grass alongside the roadway. Winter had been left behind in New York.

The events of the night before continued to flash across her mind as they had done since she first awakened. She kept seeing Jason's eyes glinting in the candlelight, the flash of his smile in the darkened room, and she could feel his hard body pressing against hers. She was having trouble reconciling her behavior last night with her carefully planned approaches to Jason. Everything had seemed so clear-cut in her mind before she actually saw him. After that...

At least the night had proved one thing to Kristi—her ice princess nickname was not appropriate. Because of her aversion to the groping and pawing most men felt to be their inalienable right, she'd convinced herself that she deserved her reputation. If it hadn't been for her memories of Jason she would have thought herself incapable of passion. After last night she knew better. Unfortunately, her responsiveness seemed to extend only to Jason McAlister.

Jason McAlister. Kristi couldn't remember the first time she saw him. He had always been a part of her life. Her mother once told her that the ten-year-old Jason had been completely captivated by his best friend's baby sister. At eleven, Kyle had had better things to do than waste time on a tiny baby with rosy wisps of hair framing her face, but Jason was fascinated by her. By the time she could walk, Kristi had become a tiny shadow following Kyle and Jason around. She remembered hearing her mother tease Jason that Kristi thought he was another brother, but Jason hadn't seemed to mind. Being an only child was lonely business and he spent more time at the Cole ranch than on his own, which adjoined theirs.

Kyle and Kristi lost their parents when she was nine. Kyle and Francine had only been married a few months when Jeremy and Carla Cole died in a multicar collision near Dallas. Kyle, Francine and Jason had tenderly enfolded the nine-year-old with their love and caring, actively seeking to fill the gap left in her life.

One particular day lingered in her memory of that time....

"I finished all my chores, Kyle! You promised I could go with you and Jase if I finished my chores." A boot-shod foot stamped the loose dirt of the barnyard as Kristi glared up at her brother. "You promised!"

An amused Jason watched the ten-year-old Kristi stand up to her brother. "C'mon, Kyle. A promise is a promise. If you told her she could go, let's get moving." Jase turned and vaulted onto his horse, impatient to be gone.

Kyle glanced back at the house as though hoping Francine would come to his rescue. He had promised and he knew it. "Hurry and get your hat, then, while I saddle Misty for you."

Kristi ran to the house but was back in moments, her hat on her head.

"Glad to be out of school for the summer?" Jason asked Kristi as she moved her horse alongside his.

"You bet. I hate being cooped up inside all day." She laughed up at him. "Wanna race?"

He grinned at her exuberance. "Not today, little one. Kyle and I stayed out late last night. I don't feel up to moving too fast today."

"I know." Kristi's curls bobbed as she nodded. "Kyle really caught it from Francine over breakfast. She said you're a bad influence on him."

"Kristi, you don't have to repeat all the family secrets," Kyle interrupted with exasperation. Glancing at his friend with a sheepish grin, he added, "Jason already knows what kind of an influence he is."

It took several years for Kristi to appreciate the strain Kyle had been placed under when their parents had died, leaving him total responsibility for the ranch and his sister, as well as a new wife. She came to realize, also, how much Kyle had depended on Jason's encouragement and support.

"Look, Kyle. I see a stray over there," Kristi had yelled as she dug her heels into the sides of her horse. Her sharp eyes had spotted the first of several they found in the course of the day.

Perhaps her memories of that day remained so vivid because it was the last day the three of them spent together for six years. A few weeks later Jason had announced that he was going into the Army. She remembered that Kyle had tried to talk him out of it, pointing out how much he was needed at his own ranch. His dad was in poor health and Jason was his only son.

"You won't get drafted, Jase. You're needed at home...just as I am." Kristi heard the note of pleading in Kyle's voice. Jason, being Jason, refused to change his mind once it was made up. He'd gone off to fight a war in a country no one had heard of ten years before.

Kristi grew up while he was away. At sixteen she looked like a woman, but inside she was still the young girl who worshiped her brother and Jason.

Over the years she had let her hair grow instead of keeping it in short curls. Those curls became long waves cascading to her waist when she wore it down, which was seldom. Instead, Kristi wore braids, despite the ribbing she got from her classmates. Braids were not part of the "in" look, but she didn't care.

She had just finished bathing one evening and was trying to dry her hair when she heard Kyle's shout. "Jason! You ole son of a gun! How the hell are you, man?" She heard the laughing response as she dashed down the long hallway to the kitchen. She barely got a glimpse of the tall, too thin man standing there before she hurled herself into his arms.

"Oh, Jase— You're home! You've finally come home!"

She felt Jason stiffen. He pushed her away with a frown and stared into her face. She looked up at him with bewilderment, and his puzzled expression caused Kyle and Francine to burst out laughing.

"Don't you even recognize Kristi any more, Jase?" Kyle's lopsided grin failed to disguise his pride in his sister's beauty.

"Kristi?" Jason's hands framed her face as he stared down at her in amazement. She swallowed and nodded, embarrassed that he had not recognized her. "My God, Kristi, you've grown up." His tone was one of amazement and more than a little dismay.

She tried to cover her discomfiture. "Well, what did you expect?" She glanced over his face, noting the new lines, the haunted expression. "And you've grown old!" With her hands resting on his shoulders she leaned up and kissed him softly on the lips and murmured, "I still love you, though." She cocked her head, waiting for his reaction with wide-eyed innocence.

He carefully removed her hands from around his neck and stepped back. His face showed his shock at the changes in her. "Yeah, well, don't let your boyfriend hear you say that, love. We can't have him getting jealous of an old man like me." He moved away from her and sat down at the table where Francine had placed coffee and cinnamon rolls.

They sat around the table for hours that night, trying to catch up on six years. Jason had lost his father three years before, and the ranch had been run by the foreman who had been there when Jason was born. "Hell," he told Kyle, "Nate does a better job of running the place than I do, anyway. He and Molly have done a great job of keeping everything going for me."

Kristi noticed that he was reticent when their questions turned to the Orient and the war. His stories centered around leaves he'd taken and the amusing incidents that occur when different cultures attempt to communicate. Kristi sat enthralled, watching the expressions on Jason's face, noticing how serious he looked when he wasn't talking, how thin he was.

The first time she rode over to see Jason his face looked like a thundercloud as he approached her. "What the hell are you doing here?" His greeting certainly wasn't an auspicious start to the renewal of their friendship.

The sorrel she rode came close to matching the color of the braid tossed over her shoulder. She looked down at him from her position in the saddle, wondering why he looked so angry as he stood there, hands on his hips, waiting for her response.

"I came to visit you, Jase. Why? Is something wrong?"

"There certainly is, you little idiot. You have no business coming over here on your own. What's wrong with Kyle, anyway, letting you come over here?"

Kristi drew herself up to her full height in the saddle and in haughty tones replied, "For your information, Jason McAlister, I'm almost seventeen years old. Much too old to need Kyle's permission before I go anywhere."

Jason jerked the battered hat from his head and popped it against his leg. Tawny hair fell across his forehead as he rubbed his forearm across his face, wiping the moisture on the sleeve of his blue chambray workshirt.

"Let me tell you something, young lady. Your brother may find you all grown up and able to look after yourself, but I sure as hell don't and I don't want you riding over here by yourself again, is that clear?" His eyes flashed as he took in her outraged expression.

He looked dangerous and she decided she didn't want to cross him. Changing tactics, she smiled with beguiling innocence. "I just wanted to come see you, Jase, what's wrong with that?"

He shook his head as he took her reins from her and led her horse to the barn. "All right, Kristi, you win for now. C'mon in the house, Molly's got lunch waiting for me or you'd never have found me." He watched her swing out of the saddle with no expression on his face. However, Kristi was relieved when he threw a companionable arm around her shoulders as they walked across the yard to the large, rambling house.

"Molly, hope you have plenty. We have company for lunch." Jason stopped just inside the doorway, his arm still around Kristi's shoulders. Molly, not much more than five feet tall, spun around from the stove with a smile.

"You know I always make enough to feed a crew of hungry men, Jase." She smiled politely at Kristi, then exclaimed, "Kristi! I almost didn't recognize you. How have you been, child?"

"Just fine, Molly."

Molly reached for another plate and began to arrange the table. Her weight did not keep her from moving lightly on her feet and she turned to Kristi with a hug. "My! Aren't you a beauty!" She glanced up. "Isn't she, Jase?"

His eyes narrowed as the two women waited for his comment. He shrugged with male nonchalance and moved toward the table. "Not nearly as beautiful as that table loaded with home cooking. Let's eat. I've got a lot of work to do before I can call it a day."

The two women looked at each other, puzzled at his response. Not that Kristi cared what she looked like or what Jason thought of her looks. She just couldn't get used to so many changes in him. It appeared that it would take them some time to regain their closeness.

The following months taught Kristi something about the unpredictability of human behavior. Jason made it clear that she would not be welcome over at his place unless accompanied by Kyle, Francine or both of them, yet he and Kyle seemed to have renewed their friendship and were closer than ever.

Jase had supper with them at least twice a week and it was those nights that convinced Kristi that not only was Jason no longer interested in having her as a friend, he didn't even like her. He would joke and kid with Kyle and Francine, but he maintained an aloof and polite distance from Kristi. She sometimes wondered if he even knew she was at the table.

Kristi remembered the night she had discovered just how aware of her he was. Jason had been home for almost a year and, as usual, had dinner with them. Also, as usual, he had ignored Kristi. After dinner, the men had gone out to the barn to look at a new foal while Kristi helped Francine with the kitchen. They were unaware that Kristi had prepared the meal they had devoured with gusto. She had made Francine promise not to tell them.

"But why not, I'd like to know? You've turned into a great cook. It seems to me you'd be proud of it!"

"I just don't want them to know," Kristi insisted stubbornly.

"Have you ever given a thought to how I feel about accepting all their compliments?" Francine asked. "It's the same as telling a lie and you know it."

"No, it isn't. I can enjoy their compliments just as much as if they were being paid to me." Kristi walked over to the door and stared out into the night. "I don't want Jason to think I'm trying to impress him."

Francine's lack of response caused Kristi to glance around. Francine stood at the sink, her expression startled. Her eyes took in the casual picture Kristi made standing in the doorway. Her eyes met Kristi's. "You love him, don't you?" Francine asked softly.

"Haven't I always?"

Francine waved the thought away. "I don't mean your hero worship of him as a kid. I mean, you really are in love with him."

Kristi didn't like the look of concern creeping across Francine's face. She shrugged. "So what? He doesn't even know I exist. But that's all right with me, too! Who needs him, anyway?"

Francine sat down in one of the chairs by the table. "Oh, Kristi, honey, I'm sorry. I should have realized."

"Oh, for God's sake, Francine. You're acting like I just contracted an incurable disease or something. I'm sure I'll survive." Her chin tilted slightly, daring Francine to disagree with her assessment of her condition.

Francine managed a faint grin. "Oh, I'm not worried about you surviving, honey. I'm more worried about Jase."

Kristi flew across the room and leaned against the table as she glared at Francine. "What's that supposed to mean?"

"Nothing insulting, so you can come off your high horse. I just have a feeling that if you really put your mind to bewitching a person, he wouldn't have a chance, and that includes Jason."

Kristi's frown grew deeper. "I still don't know what you're talking about."

"I'm talking about life, honey, and what you want to make of it." Francine got out of her chair and grabbed a cup from the cabinet. Pouring herself a cup of coffee, she continued, "My mother once told me that I should be very careful about what I wanted out of life, because I might get it." She saw the puzzled look on Kristi's face and smiled. "Like you, I didn't understand what she was talking about." She paused, gazing around the room, her eyes lingering on the colorful calendar hanging on the wall by the table. "Now I do."

She studied the young girl sitting across from her, and sighed. "I suppose your one dream in life is to marry Jase, raise kids and help him on the ranch. Am I right?"

Kristi felt consumed with embarrassment. Had she been that obvious? Was that why Jason continued to ignore her? How humiliating. She would never be able to face him again! With her head down, Kristi muttered, "How did you know?"

Francine reached over and took Kristi's hand. "Because I had the very same dream the first time I laid eyes on Kyle, that's how I know."

The tension in Kristi's shoulders eased. Maybe Jason didn't know, after all. Maybe it was just something women knew about each other that they didn't tell the menfolks.

"Does it show? My feelings for him, I mean?"

Francine patted her hand. "No, Kristi, it doesn't show. In fact, I only guessed tonight, although I should have realized why you found his attitude toward you so upsetting." She smiled. "I'm sorry it took me so long."

Restless, Kristi jumped up and strode to the refrigerator. Opening the door, she took out a pitcher of iced tea and filled a large glass. "I don't really think I expect him to be in love with me or anything, Francie. It's just that before he went away he at least seemed to like me and not mind when I tagged along.'' She took a large gulp of tea and almost choked. "Now, he acts like he can hardly stand to have me around."

"Have you taken a look at yourself in the mirror lately, Kristi?'' Francine's question seemed to have nothing to do with the conversation.

"What does that have to do with anything?"

"Plenty. When Jase went away, you were a child. He returned to find a beautiful woman in the child's place. He hasn't had time to adjust to the change.''

"How much time does he need?'' Kristi wailed.

"As much time as he wants, honey. You can't rush things like that. In your case, I'm glad."

When she had finished her tea, Kristi rinsed out her glass and set it on the drain. "You seem to be talking in riddles tonight, Francie. I just don't understand you.'' She returned to her chair and sank into it as though giving up the effort to understand.

"My dream to marry Kyle was fine for me. It was all I could ever hope for. But you,

Kristi, have so much more than most people. Don't you understand yet just what your stunning looks can do for you?'' She paused when Kristi shook her head in disgust. "I mean it. You have a sexy innocence that advertising people would love to use to sell every product known to man. Would you want to waste that potential as a rancher's wife?''

Kristi shook her head as though weary of the conversation. "Francine, you've been reading too many romances. How would someone like me, living in the back of beyond, manage to interest anybody in my looks? I can't even interest Jase.'' She stood up and wandered to the door. "I think I'll go find the men—see what they're up to.''

As her eyes adjusted to the dark Kristi saw the glow of a cigarette and headed toward it. "Kyle? Did Jase leave?'' She stopped by the tall shadow of a man leaning against the wooden fence.

"No, Jase didn't leave,'' a husky voice answered.

"Oh, hi, Jase.'' She attempted a casual tone. "Where's Kyle?'' She leaned against the fence. The moon was beginning to peek over the eastern ridge of hills, gradually shedding light over the landscape.

"He wanted to talk to some of the men about tomorrow's work. Said he'd be back in a bit." Jason dropped the butt of his cigarette and ground it out with the heel of his boot.

"You never used to smoke, Jase, before you went away." Her voice was hesitant, almost afraid of offending him.

She could hear the smile in his voice. "I know. I do a lot of things now I didn't do back then."

The warm tone reassured her. "Such as?" she asked.

He laughed. The sound sent chills down Kristi's spine. He had to have the sexiest laugh of any man she'd ever known. "They're not for the ears of innnocent little girls like you."

His teasing nettled her. "I hardly think five feet eight inches makes me a 'little girl,' Jason. Try again."

His low voice drawled from the darkness. "Then how about an innocent young girl. Is that better?"

He was laughing at her. He never took her seriously and she resented it. She was surprised to hear herself murmur in a low tone,

"What makes you think I'm so innocent,
Jase?" Thank God it was too dark for him to
see her flaming face. Whatever had possessed
her to respond in such a manner? Good grief,
she'd never even been on a date that wasn't
part of a group get-together. At those times
she'd shown no interest in experimenting with
the opposite sex.

She realized that Jase had taken her remark
seriously when he moved toward her and
pulled her into his arms. Her gasp was muffled by his lips as they moved over her mouth.
His kiss stunned her. It bore no relation to the
loving kisses exchanged in her family. Then,
suddenly, he lifted his head. "That's what
makes me think you're an innocent, Kristi," he
mocked. "You don't even know how to kiss."

Kristi's anger overcame her embarrassment, and before Jason could move away from
her, she wrapped her arms about his neck,
pulling herself up close to him, her small
breasts pressed tightly against his hard chest.
She could feel the beat of his heart as it
marched double time. *Good*, she thought. *He
won't have it all his own way.* "Why don't you
teach me?" she asked as she touched her lips
to his.

She could feel his body tense at her bold action. His firm mouth thinned under her lips and she could feel his arms moving to her wrists to remove them from around his neck. In an act of desperation, she ran her tongue over his lips, stroking them in quick, kitten-like licks. He froze at her audacious move, his mouth parting in surprise. Kristi's lips molded themselves hungrily to his.

Jason's arms came around her in a squeezing grip as he began to respond. She felt, more than heard, his amused chuckle as his kiss replied to her invitation. His mouth searched out all of her tender areas—he nibbled on her lobes, breathing softly in her ear. His lips traced a line over her cheek and returned to her mouth in a possession that made her forget where they were and why.

As her body reacted to his, Kristi began to imitate his moves, her tongue dueling with his, her hands stroking his back as she moved closer to him. She became aware of his arousal and her breath caught in her throat. *His body knows he's holding a woman in his arms, even if his brain refuses to admit it.*

Pleased with the thought, Kristi let her mind go blank and began to enjoy the new sensations taking over her body.

Jase shifted so that his legs carried both their weights as Kristi leaned against him, lost in the passion he'd so unexpectedly stirred within her. She could not get enough of him and wanted to learn all he could teach her. The slamming of the screen door startled them. Jason jerked his head away from her. Kristi stood there with her eyes closed, feeling suddenly cold without his warm lips possessing hers.

He whispered, "I'm sorry, Kristi. I don't know what I was thinking of." She could feel the moonlight touching them, surrounding them with a magic silver cloak. Her eyelids slowly fluttered open and she gazed into his face, which was half in shadow.

"Jase?" she asked in a wondering voice. She had just received her first taste of the sensual pleasure she had pretended to know already. She'd had no idea her body was capable of such feelings.

"You'd better get on into the house, Kristi. I need to get home myself." His voice was cool, as though he was unaffected by what had just happened. Kristi knew better. She was still close enough to hear his uneven breathing. Her hand was resting on his chest and she could feel his heart racing. Why was he trying to deny what had happened between them?

"What's wrong, Jason? Didn't you want to kiss me?" She was puzzled and hurt by his reaction.

"I'm too old to be playing kissing games in the dark, Kristi." His voice sounded harsh. "Why don't you do your experimenting with someone your own age?"

She stepped back as though he had slapped her. She'd made a complete fool of herself, throwing herself at him like that. Pride came to her rescue. "Now why didn't I think of that? Maybe I will." She spun away from him and stomped toward the house.

It was a long time before Kristi slept that night.

Kristi graduated from high school two weeks after her eighteenth birthday. As far as she was concerned, she was through with school forever. She'd enjoyed parts of it—the English, history, speech and art classes, and she'd hated parts of it—the math and science classes and phys. ed. She'd made good grades, but she was glad to have school behind her.

When she tried to talk to Kyle about taking on more responsibility around the ranch, he was vague in his responses, but he allowed her to spend most of her days with him as she had during the past summers.

Francine felt that Kristi could have a career as a model. She decided to have pictures of Kristi made and insisted on driving all the way to Dallas to a professional photographer. She explained to Kristi that she wanted pictures of her at that age, but Kristi thought the whole trip a waste of time. The photographer spent hours with her, having her change from casual wear to formal, all of which Francine just happened to have with them, but Kristi balked at donning her two-piece swimsuit.

"No way, Francine. You can remember me with clothes on, or not at all." The photographer and Francine exchanged looks, and Francine shrugged, knowing that was one battle she wouldn't win.

Kristi had her own plans. Ever since that night in the spring when Jason had kissed her, she had considered what she should do about him. He was not indifferent to her—she had discovered that, but she was uncertain how to use the information. One thing was certain, by the end of the summer Jason McAlister would see her as a woman!

First of all, she knew she had to convince him that she wasn't too young for him. What was ten years' difference, anyway? Especially if they both were adults. She knew she wouldn't convince him of her maturity if she made calf eyes at him every time he saw her. So she began a subtle campaign to convince Jason that she saw him only as a friend, nothing more.

After months of observing his wariness around her, she was heartened to notice that he was beginning to relax and treat her in much the same way he treated Francine.

Kristi had been out of school a couple of months when she made her next move.

"Kyle, could I borrow the station wagon to go into Cielo? There's a movie I've wanted to see for ages and tonight's the last night." Her eyes held all the starry-eyed innocence of youth as she looked first at her brother, then at Francine, and glanced quickly at Jason before she looked down at her plate. Dinner was almost over.

Kyle frowned. "Kristi, I've never known you to want to drive into town this late at night. It would be after midnight by the time you got out, then you'd have that long drive home." He looked to Francine for support.

"Kristi, if you want to see a show tonight, I could take you, if you'd like." Jason's voice sounded casual and friendly, nothing more.

Kristi looked up, surprised. "Oh, thanks, Jase, but that's okay. If Kyle doesn't mind my using the old car, I'll be fine." She finished the remaining food on her plate, then looked back at Kyle. "I'll be all right, you know."

Kyle frowned, then cleared his throat. "Uh, Kristi, I don't want to sound hard-nosed about this, but I'd be much happier if you'd let Jase take you into town. You could have car trouble or something and I'd really worry about you." His eyes begged for her understanding of his position.

Oh, how she loved her brother! She was almost sorry she'd put him through all of this. Glancing down at her empty plate, then ruefully at Jason, she smiled. "I'm sorry, Jase. I didn't mean to be rude. If you're willing to take me, that will be fine." Kyle's sigh of relief echoed around the kitchen.

As it happened, the movie turned out to be a double feature. The first one, a western, kept them both entertained. The second movie, a love story that reduced Kristi to tears at the end, moved Jason as well.

By the time they left the theater, the town was closed. They returned to Jason's truck, in silence and drove toward home. To comfort her, Jason pulled Kristi over to his side and drove with one arm, keeping the other one firmly around her shoulders. Kristi let her head drop onto Jason's shoulder, her mind still on the movie. Only gradually did she become aware of the musky smell of his after-shave, of the muscles of his thigh bunched beneath her hand. She hadn't realized how natural it was for her hand to rest there. His fingers drew soft designs on her arm and she shifted a little closer to him and spoke softly into his ear.

"Do you realize this is the first time we've been alone together in months?" Her breath brushed softly against his ear. She noticed his shiver.

Removing his arm from around her, he reached into his pocket for a cigarette. She punched the lighter on the dash and waited, then held it to his cigarette.

After it was lit, he moved both hands back to the wheel. "I know."

She waited, but he said nothing more. "Are you still angry about that night?"

"What night?"

"The night I kissed you."

"I thought we both did a pretty good job of kissing each other," he replied, a hint of humor in his voice.

She laughed. "Yes, I guess we did at that. Anyway, I'm sorry my behavior caused you to steer clear of me after that." She watched his profile, mentally tracing the strong nose and jawline, wishing she were an artist who could portray the strength in him.

"That isn't the reason I've been avoiding you," he said in a low tone.

Her heart did a flip. He'd admitted that it had been intentional. "Oh?" She tried to sound uncaring. "What was your reason, then?"

His eyes cut quickly to her face, barely discernible in the light from the dash. "I knew I wouldn't be able to keep my hands off you, so I stayed away." He dragged deeply on his cigarette, then leaned over and put it out.

"But now you've discovered you can?"

"What do you think? Didn't I behave myself at the movie?" His grin slanted across his face, causing Kristi's breathing to do strange things.

"Did you find my crush very embarrassing, Jase?"

"Your crush? I don't know what you're talking about."

"Of course you do. All my fantasies have been about you. Surely you knew that?" She watched his face for a reaction but saw none.

"That's okay, honey. Because all my fantasies since I got back home have sure as hell been about you!" He reached out and pulled her back to his side. He leaned over and whispered as he watched the road, "I would have been thrown out of the movie tonight if they had known some of the fantasies I was having about you."

Kristi started laughing. "Oh, Jase. This is crazy. If that's the way you feel, why haven't you said anything?"

"I've been waiting for you to grow up, Kristi, as patiently as I know how."

"Don't look now, Jason, but you done missed it." She leaned over and kissed him on the ear. "Not only am I now eighteen years old, but I'm a high school graduate—ready to meet the world.''

He slowed the truck as he turned off the highway and took the farm road that led to their respective homes. "What do you want to do now that you're out of school?''

"Love you.''

Her quiet reply startled him so much that his foot slipped from the accelerator and the truck suddenly slowed. After a moment, Jase put his foot on the gas pedal again. Kristi laid her head back on his shoulder, content to let him decide what to do with her statement. They rode along in silence for several miles, and Kristi was almost asleep when Jason spoke.

"What do you want to do, Kristi?''

Her head jerked up. For a minute she was uncertain whether she was dreaming or he'd actually spoken. They pulled into the drive of the ranch and he flipped off the lights and engine.

"About what, Jase?''

He turned so that he was leaning against the door and facing her. "About us.''

She had never heard him more serious and Kristi's heart lurched at his acknowledgment that there was an "us.''

She grinned, feeling more sure of herself with Jason than she ever had. "What do you have in mind?" Her teasing tone caught him on the quick.

"I want to take you somewhere and love you until you cry for help." His tone sounded almost grim.

She tilted her head. "Fine. How about next weekend?"

He jerked upright. "Are you serious?"

"Sure. Aren't you? I can tell Francine I'm spending the weekend in town with a friend... only I'll spend it with you."

Jason couldn't see the panicky expression in her eyes as she heard herself blithely plan a stolen weekend with him. All he heard was her light, casual tone.

"You see nothing wrong in going off with me for a weekend?" His tone was carefully neutral.

Kristi was glad he was no longer touching her because her whole body shook with every heartbeat. She loved this man too much and had loved him too long to turn back now. "No, not if you want me."

"Oh, I want you, Kristi, never doubt that." He pulled her into his arms, ignoring the steering wheel that suddenly poked Kristi in the ribs. His kiss made no allowance for her youth or lack of experience as he proceeded to show her how much he wanted her. Only her gasp of pain as the steering wheel continued to gouge her side caused him to ease his grip on her. "This is obviously not the place for this," he muttered with disgust.

Kristi sat back, trying to get her breath, hoping the panicky feeling would go away. This was Jason, and she loved him. That was all that mattered.

It was easy to get away for the weekend. When she told Francine she was spending the weekend in town with a friend, Francine commented that she must be getting bored with ranch life already. Kristi ignored the comment, knowing better but unable to explain.

Kristi had never lied to her family and they trusted her completely. Not even Kyle was suspicious when Jason arrived to give her a lift into town.

"Where are we going?" They had been driving for miles and Jase had said nothing; he had just stared down the road, frowning.

"Nuevo Laredo."

"Mexico?"

He heard the shock in her voice and glanced at her for a moment before returning his eyes to the road. "What's wrong with Mexico?"

"Oh, I don't know. I guess I was just surprised."

"Where did you think I'd take you? To my place, for Molly to look after us?" He sounded angry, which wasn't a good sign for the weekend.

"I wasn't thinking, Jase. Anywhere is fine."

They continued to travel in silence. This wasn't how Kristi had imagined their time together. Not that she had any intention of changing her mind, but she thought Jase would be more relaxed so she could be. After all, he probably did this sort of thing all the time. A pain shot through her at the thought. She tried to shrug it off. He was twenty-eight years old; she couldn't expect him to have reached that age without experience. She just preferred not to think about it.

Kristi's surprised turned to alarm when, after crossing into Mexico, instead of looking for a hotel, Jason stopped in front of an official-looking building. "Where are we?"

Jason turned to her, a determined expression on his face. "Kristi, I'm not going to sneak off with you for a weekend in a motel, then casually return you to Kyle. I thought I could do it, since it was obviously what you want, but I can't."

Kristi's heart plummeted to her toes. She should have known that he didn't find her attractive enough, that he'd been amusing himself at her expense. So why had he stopped here?

In the same determined voice, Jason continued. "We're going inside, Kristi, and we're getting married." He held up a hand as she started to speak. "I don't want to hear any arguments, dammit. I love you, and there's no way in hell I'm going to be able to make love to you and then walk away. We're getting married, and when we get back I'll tell Kyle and Francine what we've done. They're going to be upset, and I'm sorry we're doing it this way—" he paused, reaching out to her cheek as though unable to resist touching her "—but I've waited too long for you now to wait until we can plan a big wedding."

"Oh, Jase!" Kristi threw herself into his arms, oblivious to the passersby and their curious stares. She began to kiss him—quick kisses across his cheeks, eyes and nose—

laughing at his startled expression. "I never dreamed you'd want to marry me, Jase. I was willing to accept whatever you offered. Of course I want to marry you, you crazy idiot. That's all I've ever wanted out of life."

As they walked into the building hand in hand, he muttered, "I still feel like a sneak."

"That's because you are," she admitted as she hugged his arm to her. "And a thief, stealing your best friend's little sister." She laughed, happiness radiating from her.

His indulgent smile made her want to weep. "I'm not stealing, just borrowing."

They spent the weekend in a luxurious Mexican hotel.

Nothing in Kristi's experience prepared her for Jason's lovemaking. He recognized her nervousness and didn't rush her. If he had any doubts because she was so young she quickly disabused him of them. She was ready to learn more about the sensual side of her nature and he was the one she wanted to teach her. Her love for him grew as he took the time and patience to show her how beautiful lovemaking could be.

During the daytime they enjoyed touring the shops and marketplace, and they eagerly embraced the custom of siesta time, although they got very little rest.

They intended to leave early on Sunday so they would have plenty of time to talk with Kyle and Francine, but even with the best intentions, they continued to be distracted during the process of showering, dressing and packing, and it was midafternoon before they pulled up at the ranch.

Kristi was nervous. With her marriage a fact, she began to worry that perhaps she wasn't prepared for marriage and all it entailed. Although she eagerly looked forward to moving in with Jason, she was unsure about what he might expect of her as his wife.

Jason and Kristi walked into the living room and paused inside the door. Kyle was stretched out on the couch watching television while Francine, in her third month of pregnancy, busily crocheted something tiny and intricate.

Kristi was the first to speak. "Kyle, Francine...we've got something to tell you." She paused as Kyle rolled to a sitting position, then, seeing Jason, stood up and stretched.

He grinned at his friend. "H'lo, Jason. Didn't know you were here. What did you do, go all the way into town to pick up Kristi?"

"Not exactly," Jason drawled. "I never dropped her off, Kyle. Kristi and I were married on Friday."

Kyle froze in his position as though caught in the frame of a moving picture, his arm raised to push his reddish brown hair from his forehead, a half-formed smile stranded on his face.

"Oh, no!" Francine jumped up, yarn, pattern and needle falling unheeded to the floor. "Oh, Kristi, you didn't!" She looked stricken and Kristi felt a pang of remorse as she quickly moved to Francine's side.

"Oh, Francie, I'm sorry we didn't tell you, but we didn't really decide to do it until Friday, and then it was done." She put her arms around the smaller woman. "Please don't cry, Francie. You know this is what I've always wanted."

Kyle suddenly regained movement and straightened to his full height, a couple of inches taller than Jason. He shifted toward the younger man, anger warring with pain on his face.

"Is there some particular reason you had to be in such an all-fired hurry, Jase?" His penetrating blue eyes speared his friend, as he waited for an explanation.

Kristi watched the color wash over Jason's cheeks. He wasn't the kind of man to explain himself to anyone, but Kyle was different. No two men had ever been closer. "No, Kyle, there wasn't the kind of reason you're implying. You know me better than that."

"I thought I knew you better than that, but the Jason McAlister I knew wouldn't have snuck off with my sister without a word, either." Kristi had never seen her brother so upset, not since they had lost their parents.

She left Francine and threw herself into Kyle's arms. "Please don't be upset, Kyle. I couldn't stand that. I love Jason, you've always known that. Our getting married was an impulsive decision, that's true, but it would have happened, anyway. Jason is all I've ever wanted out of life. I was marking time until he decided to see me as an adult."

"From the sound of things, he managed to do that," Kyle responded with an attempt at humor. He held out his hand to Jason. "I guess at this point all I need to do is welcome you to the family, which seems a little strange. You've always been that." He gripped his friend's hand, and they stood there looking at each other, neither one willing to be the first to end eye contact.

"Oh, Kristi, I had such great plans for you, too," Francine wailed as she picked up the items she'd dropped. "I've sent all those pictures to a New York agent in hopes of getting you into a modeling school."

Both Jason and Kristi turned to her in surprise. Jason was the first to speak. "What are you talking about, Francie?"

"I took Kristi to Dallas and had a portfolio of pictures taken several weeks ago. Everyone who knows anything about the business says she's a natural with her unusual coloring and skin tones, not to mention those eyes. I've just been waiting to hear from the agent before I said anything to Kristi."

Jason's eyes hardened as he turned and stared at Kristi. "I didn't know you wanted to be a model, Kristi. You never mentioned it."

Kristi was appalled to see the cold, aloof Jason where her warm and passionate husband had been just a few minutes before. She moved over to him and slid her arms around his waist. Gazing up at him, she tried to make him understand. "I don't, Jason. This is the first time I knew anything about such plans."

"You posed for the pictures."

"Francie said she wanted some pictures of me. I had no idea she intended to use them for anything but to have here at home."

Francine spoke up. "That's true, Jason. It was my idea. I felt that Kristi has too much potential to waste on a ranch." She faced her new brother-in-law with spirit, determined not to back down.

Kristi broke the tension in the room by leaning into Jason and kissing him in the V of his shirt. "You're all I want, Jason. Haven't I made that plain enough this weekend?"

She could feel his body's response to her closeness and gloried in her ability to affect him. Her power over this man was new and fascinating. When she glanced up at him she recognized the desire that darkened his topaz eyes. "It's just as well, Kristi, because it's too late to change your mind now. You're my wife. You said that was what you wanted and I believed you." His arms encircled her in a possessive hug as he spoke to her, both of them absorbed in each other and unaware of the other two in the room. "You'd better go pack your things. I need to get home."

Kristi saw very little of Kyle and Francine during the next few weeks—she was too engrossed in settling into her new position as Jason's wife. Although she was an accomplished cook, she begged Molly to stay on as Jason's housekeeper, insisting she still had a lot to learn about home management. Amused, Molly consented and gently guided Kristi through the steps of running a large household.

Kristi had been living with Jason for a little over a week when the phone rang one day. "Is this Kristi Cole?"

Momentarily forgetting her new married name, she answered, "Yes."

"Kristi, this is Jonathan Segal. I've just been chatting with your sister-in-law, Francine. She was kind enough to give me your phone number."

Who in the world was Jonathan Segal? "I'm afraid I don't understand, Mr. Segal. Why did you want to contact me?"

She heard a chuckle over what sounded like a long-distance line. "Mrs. Cole explained to me that she was the one who sent me your pictures. It doesn't matter to me who sent them. I wanted to let you know that if you'd come to

New York, I think I can help you get your pretty puss on the cover of every national magazine published." He laughed. "Except, perhaps, *Field & Stream.*"

He must be the agent Francine had mentioned. "I'm sorry you had to waste the call, Mr. Segal. Surely Francine told you I'm married and not interested in a career in modeling."

There was a moment of silence as her comment was weighed and evaluated. "I see." A longer pause. "That's really too bad. You're one of the most photogenic young women to come along in a long while. You don't seem to have a bad side or angle. With your looks and my contacts, you could very easily become the highest-paid model around in a few short years."

For a moment, glamorous pictures of exotic locales and glittering showrooms flitted through Kristi's mind. Could the man be for real? Then Jason's face superimposed itself over the other imaginings and she smiled. "I appreciate your interest in me, but I'm afraid I have other commitments now."

She heard his sigh winging across the wires. "All right. But, Kristi, if you should ever change your mind, please give me a call."

She laughed. "I'll do that, Mr. Segal. If I ever decide to become rich and famous, you'll be the first person I notify."

"You think it's a joke at the moment, my friend, but that's exactly what I can do for you. Just keep it in mind."

As the months passed, Kristi forgot the call. She became too caught up in the problems that seemed to be appearing in her marriage. Jason began to spend time away from the ranch, but would give no explanations to Kristi as to why.

She was still awake late one night when he carefully climbed into bed beside her. It was almost two o'clock and her imagination had been torturing her with pictures of Jason with another woman, or in a car wreck, or out drinking with his buddies while she waited for him at home. Was he bored with her already?

"Where have you been?" She'd been determined not to let him know she was awake. Where was her self-discipline?

He pulled her into his arms, his hands roving leisurely over her body, seeming to enjoy the curves his palms outlined so faithfully. "At a meeting. It ran a little later than I expected. I would have called, but I was afraid I would wake you." He began to kiss her just below her ear, an action that he'd discovered guaranteed her full attention.

"You didn't mention having anything planned at supper," she murmured, recognizing that, as usual, his hands and mouth were seducing her to forget her tension and unease.

"I didn't know about it then. The call came later."

"What kind of meeting, Jase? What's so important that you drop everything every time you receive a phone call and go rushing off?" She moved her mouth slightly to avoid his and heard him sigh.

"I'm sorry, Kristi, but I can't talk about it. Don't let it come between us." She heard the tenderness in his voice and melted against him, knowing she could never resist him for long.

His secret meetings did come between them. As the months passed he began to stay away for a night or two at a time. He was always careful to let her know when he'd be gone, and he made sure that Nate and Molly were around to look after her. Kristi grew more frustrated as time went on. Why did he have to be so secretive? Why did he continue to treat her like a child? Maybe not exactly a child—more like a pampered plaything, waiting to fall into his arms every time he returned. She had a disgusting habit of doing just that.

Perhaps in time Kristi would have overcome her insecurities as a new bride and continued her life with Jason if she hadn't lost their baby. She'd been so excited when she found out she was pregnant. Francine had given birth to Kevin only a few weeks before and she was delighted to think they would both have babies near the same age. Jason treated her as though she were suddenly made of priceless porcelain, and life began to seem much more worthwhile to Kristi. However, he continued to disappear periodically with little warning and still refused to tell her why.

Kristi was in her twelfth week of pregnancy when, during one of the nights Jason was gone, she woke up suddenly, realizing that something was drastically wrong. Panicked, she flipped on the lamp by the bed, reached for the phone and called her brother. He and Francine arrived within minutes.

Kristi remembered very little about that night, but clearly recalled the details of the next morning when the compassionate, white-haired doctor took her hand and explained that she had lost the baby she and Jason had been awaiting so eagerly. The doctor patted her hand as he made his explanations.

"There were complications during the surgery we had to do, Kristi. It's hard to predict the outcome of some of these things, you know." His eyes had the sad look of one who had seen too much to believe that everything always worked out for the best. "There's a strong possibility that you won't be able to have children, Kristi. Only time will tell."

She heard his voice and saw his lips form the words, but her mind rejected what he was trying to tell her.

"No! That isn't so. Jase and I plan to have a big family. He hated being an only child. We're going to have lots of children, Doctor. I've already told you." She grabbed his hand and squeezed it as though to force him to acknowledge that he was wrong.

He nodded his head. "I know, Kristi. There's still a chance. I just thought it better to prepare you in case things don't turn out quite as you planned."

He sat there with her as she broke down and cried—for her lost baby, and for the ones who might never come—then cried again because it was the doctor who sat by her side comforting her, when all she wanted in the world was Jason.

Only Jason wasn't there.

It was long after visiting hours that night before he tiptoed into her room. Kristi had been lying there staring at the reflection of the night-light. The cover was fluted, causing a flowerlike silhouette on the wall. She turned her head at the slight sound of the door closing and watched him come toward the bed. He knelt down beside her, his arms going around her as he placed his head on her chest and held her in silence. Her hand moved up to his tawny hair and her fingers gently combed through it.

When he raised his head, she saw the wet sheen of his golden eyes as he leaned down and kissed her gently on her lips. "I'm so sorry, Kristi," he whispered.

"I know," she murmured, glad to have him back even while she wondered how long he'd stay before disappearing once again.

"Has the doctor said how long you have to stay?"

"I can leave in the morning. He wanted to make sure I didn't start hemorrhaging again."

He started to speak and his voice broke. He tried again. "I should have been there with you." There was nothing she could say to that.

In the weeks that followed, Kristi found less and less to say as she began to retreat from the pain of her loss and her bewilderment about Jason. He appeared to love her and his desire for her was evident every time he was within touching distance, but she could no longer cope with the complexities of her new adult world.

It was during one of Jason's absences that Kristi remembered Jonathan Segal. For whatever his reasons, Jason no longer seemed to need a wife, especially one who might never have the family he wanted so badly. If she left him he could divorce her and remarry. In her depressed frame of mind Kristi felt she no longer had anything to offer him.

Jonathan Segal made it clear that she had plenty to offer the modeling business and assured her he would make all the necessary arrangements to get her into a highly prestigious school. All she needed to do was to let him know when she would be arriving.

Jason made no argument when she announced her decision to leave, but she remembered that his tan suddenly stood out on his face as though painted on. Perhaps she had hoped he would beg her to stay—she wasn't sure what she had expected—but he didn't. So she left.

Still locked in her cocoon of grief, Kristi moved to New York and began training to be a model. She met the challenge of a strict diet, stringent schedules and constant demands on her time and energy, glad to be distracted from her memories.

The sadness lurking in her eyes gave a haunting quality to her photographs. Jonathan pointed out that every man who looked at them wanted to be the one to make her eyes glow with happiness. It wasn't long before she found herself in constant demand, which was fine with her. As long as she stayed busy, she didn't have time to think.

Superficially, her social life was full. She learned to be at ease in the sophisticated circles that included many of the wealthy and the famous. She was immune to the propositions and proposals that came her way—all of her emotions had been left behind in Texas.

As the years passed she emerged from her self-imposed emotional prison and took a more active part in the direction of her life. Kristi wasn't sure exactly when she decided to cut her ties and ask Jason for a divorce. She could not bring herself to return to Texas, despite Francine's many letters importuning her to get acquainted with the rapidly growing Kevin and his younger sister, Kari. However, when her lawyer told her that Jason was proving to be most uncooperative and suggested that she might wish to discuss the divorce with him in person, Kristi knew it was time for her to face him.

There was no reason for Jason to balk—she'd made it clear that she wanted nothing from him. She just wanted to be free to live her life.

As she drove toward her brother's ranch that fresh, spring morning, remembering her night with Jason, she began to wonder if she would ever be free.

Three

Kristi had an opportunity to note the changes in the ranch as she followed the long, winding private road from the highway to the ranch buildings and the home of her childhood. She had waited a long time to return. She hoped it was long enough. Last night had shown her that Jason had a stronger hold on her than one person should have over another. Her only protection was in not letting him know.

Her car had no sooner stopped than the screen door of the house flew open and twin tornadoes burst into view. For a quick spasm of time, Kristi's heart felt squeezed by a giant hand, then the pain was gone. She was back in the present once more.

The children tore across the front porch and down the steps, then came to a screeching halt—their shyness of strangers overcoming their anticipation of meeting, at long last, their aunt.

Kristi recognized the family resemblance. Kevin, tall for almost six, was slender like his dad. He stood watching her as though hoping she'd have something for him to do. Kari, at four, showed signs of beauty. Both had their father's reddish brown hair—Francine's black curls didn't show up on either child.

They watched as Kristi stepped nimbly from the car. She smiled and asked, "Would you like to help me with some of my luggage?"

That was the invitation they needed to send them darting toward the car. Kevin took Kristi's keys and went to the trunk while Kari proudly lifted the overnight case from the front seat.

Francine joined them, hugging her sister-in-law. "Oh, Kristi, I'm so glad you came home." She hung on for a moment, struggling to keep back the tears. "It's so good to see you."

Kristi laughed, the abandoned, joyous laugh that used to echo in the old homestead. "I'm delighted to *be* home, little sister." She hugged the smaller woman back. "I'm glad to see your tribe in the flesh. They're definitely livelier than their pictures indicated."

"That's for sure. Now you can understand how difficult it was for me to get them still long enough to snap a photo."

As they walked toward the house, the children bringing up the rear, Kristi asked with a chuckle, "Are you sorry you followed Mom's idea of naming the children with a *K?*"

"I have to admit it's been confusing. Kevin is incensed when I slip and call him Kari, so I've learned to be careful."

"At least Kyle and I never had that problem. I guess Mom had gotten used to saying his name before I came along."

They walked through the side door that opened into the kitchen.

"Oh, Francie, this is beautiful. When did you have it done?"

Francine blushed with pride. "Actually, I just finished hanging the curtains when I heard your car in the drive."

Kristine remembered the kitchen, the room where most of the family congregated, as being cozy, but not particularly stylish. Now one wall was covered in red-and-white wallpaper and matching curtains hung at the windows. The cabinets were stained pecan, and the counter top echoed the bright colors of the curtains and wall.

"You're a magician," Kristi added as she smiled at her sister-in-law. She wandered over to the window that looked out on the yard. "I suppose Kyle is out somewhere on the ranch."

"Yes, but he'll be home for dinner as usual. He'll be surprised to see you. You were so vague about your plans on the phone that we had no idea when to expect you."

"I know. I didn't want a tight time schedule. One of the purposes of this trip is to rest and relax, something I've almost forgotten how to do. So I didn't push myself at all." She walked over to the large refrigerator and opened it, found the pitcher of iced tea she knew would be in there, and poured herself a glass. "What did Kyle think about my coming home?"

Francine placed some homemade cookies on a plate and motioned for Kristi to sit down at the table as she replied, "I believe his exact words were something like—" she dropped her voice to mimic her husband's husky drawl "—'it's about damn time.'" They both started laughing.

Kristi sank into one of the kitchen chairs and reached for one of Francine's fantastic cookies. She hadn't realized how much she'd missed them until now. Francine's next words suddenly jerked her back from her nostalgia. "Jason's coming over for supper tonight, Kristi." She paused, watching the expression on Kristi's face before she continued. "Unless you want me to suggest he not come."

Why did her pulse rate have to increase at the mere mention of his name? Kristi struggled to overcome her sudden nervousness. She was almost twenty-five years old, not eighteen, and had learned to handle herself with poise in the most difficult situations. Forcing herself to relax, she smiled and answered, "Oh, I don't mind his coming over, Francie. We're bound to see each other sooner or later."

She pushed the thought of the night before out of her mind. "Of course, I'm not sure how he's going to feel about seeing me again."

Francine studied Kristi, searching for the young girl she used to know in this self-contained, beautiful, young woman. She had an almost otherworld loveliness, an ethereal beauty—definitely not the stuff a rancher's wife was made of.

"Jason told us you'd had divorce papers sent to him."

"Did he?" Kristi replied in a neutral tone.

"Yes." Francine hesitated, unsure of herself with this new Kristi and conscious of past mistakes. "You know, Kristi—" she paused and licked her dry lips before continuing "—I made a vow when you left that I was going to stay out of your business. I did enough damage when I took it upon myself to contact Jonathan Segal—"

Kristi interrupted. "And you were right, you see. You were proven right, and I've never even thanked you for helping me get where I am."

"Right or wrong, I had no business butting into your life like I did. During these past few years I've kept my mouth shut—" her gaze pierced Kristi as she continued "—until now.

I think there's something you need to know, and you sure won't hear it from Kyle or Jason."

Kristi stiffened but there wasn't a thing she could do. She knew she wasn't going to like what Francine had to say. "Go on." She nodded, waiting.

"I don't know why you decided to leave Jason, Kristi, and I don't want to know. You were hurtin' pretty bad when you left Texas and maybe it was the best thing for you to do—to get away, learn something about the world, discover your own potential. Obviously it helped to heal your hurts." She leaned closer to Kristi. "Did you ever think of Jason and his pain?"

Kristi clutched the glass in her hand, staring down at the floating ice cubes as though searching for an answer written on one of them. She took a long swallow, then set the glass down on the table. "I'm sure he was hurt that I left, Francie, although he never suggested I stay."

For a moment anger flared in Francine's eyes, then it was gone as she shook her head in weary acceptance. "You just don't have a clue yet to Jason, do you, Kristi?"

"What do you mean?"

"Jason McAlister has never been able to deny you anything you ever wanted in your entire life. Why would you expect him to stop you if you decided you wanted to become a model in New York?"

"He could have said something, but he didn't. As a matter of fact he didn't have much to say about anything after we lost the baby." She moved her glass in absent circles, watching the liquid swirling.

"Kristi—I know you suffered when you lost the baby, but don't you see? Jason suffered right along with you. And he felt guilty for not being there that night, as though in some way he could have prevented it, just by being there." Francine paused, searching for words. "Then, as if that wasn't enough, he lost the wife he adored, as well. He had to stand there and watch you walk out of his life, because if that was what you wanted, he wouldn't stop you."

Kristi stood up suddenly, needing to release some of the nervous tension building within her. She moved toward the window and gazed out at the familiar view. "Then why doesn't he give me the divorce I want?" She spoke with her back to Francine, refusing to face her.

"Maybe he thought you should ask for it in person."

Kristi spun around. "That's exactly what I intend to do. That's the other reason I'm here, as I'm sure you've guessed."

Francine stood up slowly, as though all of her joints were resisting each move, almost as if she were an old woman. "Yes, I guessed as much." She watched the fey creature at the window, then decided to finish what she'd started. "I don't want you to give me the answer to this question, Kristi. It's one I think you need to answer only to yourself. Do you think you've been fair with Jase? Have you ever looked at what's happened from his point of view? Because if you haven't, I think you should."

She carried their glasses to the sink, her tone lightening. "That's all the mother-henning I intend to do, so you can relax. I want you to enjoy your stay here for however long you can be with us. You don't owe me any explanations. I don't think I'd even want to hear them." She walked over to Kristi and hugged her again. "C'mon. Let me show you your room."

Francine led the way into the hall. "I turned the spare room into a guest room so that when you decided to visit you'd have a comfortable place to stay." She paused and allowed Kristi to enter the room first.

The room at the end of the hall had always been a "catchall" room when Kristi lived there. The sewing machine, ironing board and half-completed projects of one nature or another had been stored in the room. The change in the room took her breath away.

The walls had been tinted with a soft yellow that reminded Kristi of the sky on clear mornings as it was first touched by the sun. Lace curtains covered the windows that looked out over the colorful flower garden Francine had so carefully nurtured. French provincial furniture with its touches of gold on white gave the room a feminine look. Kristi walked over to the four-poster bed and smoothed the light blue, patterned spread that was draped gracefully across it.

"Francine, you could have made a fortune as a decorator. This room is really special."

She glanced around and saw Francine's cheeks turn pink with pleasure at the compliment.

"Thank you, even if you are prejudiced. Unfortunately, I can only seem to decorate in down-home, country style, which I'm sure wouldn't impress any of your New York friends. Anyway, I'm glad you like it. I guess you can tell that I had you in mind, especially when I picked the carpet."

Kristi had already kicked off her shoes, and her bare toes curled into the thick nap of the plush, navy blue rug. "I don't suppose I can get too much blue. Thank you for thinking of me." She hadn't realized until now, when her muscles were beginning to relax, how tense she'd been. "If you don't mind, I think I'll stretch out for a few minutes."

"Sure. Kyle should be here some time within the next hour."

"If I doze off, be sure to wake me when he gets here."

Francine laughed. "Don't worry. You'll think there's a stampede let loose in the house when Kyle sees your car out front and knows you're here." She glanced out the window as she spoke. "By the way, that's a mighty fancy car you're driving, lady."

Kristi stretched out on the bed, reveling in the luxurious feel of the springy mattress. "I know. I had to have something to get away in on weekends. That car used to be my magic carpet, whisking me to upstate New York whenever I had the chance to escape."

Francine stopped by the side of the bed and touched Kristi's shoulder. "It's certainly done that for you now. It's almost as good as Dorothy's red shoes." She started out of the room, then paused and looked back. "Remember what Dorothy learned, Kristi. There's no place like home."

"Do you suppose this is Goldilocks sleeping in my bed?" Kyle's voice brought Kristi from a sound sleep. As her eyes opened she saw her brother standing by the bed, flanked by Kevin and Kari.

Kari giggled. "She's not Goldilocks, Daddy. Goldilocks has yellow hair!" Kari's blue eyes flashed up at her father.

"Hmm." Kyle rubbed his cheek as though in serious thought. "I think you're right, Kari. So who could this be?" His solemn expression was belied by the dancing eyes peering down at Kristi.

In his most adult voice Kevin explained, "It's Aunt Kristi, Daddy. Mom told you she was here."

Kristi struggled to a sitting position and smiled. "You're right, Kevin. I think your dad is trying to be funny."

"*Trying* to be funny," Kyle repeated in a wounded tone. "Boy, I thought I'd get a little more respect from you after all these years." He sat down next to Kristi and pulled her into his arms. He studied her face as he added in a suspiciously gruff voice, "Welcome home, baby sister. It's about time."

Kristi's head dropped on his shoulder. "It's good to be home, Kyle, and you're right. It's long overdue."

"You see, you and I have always agreed on the important things." He pulled her with him as he stood up. "C'mon, lunch is ready and I'm starving." The two children bounded down the hallway ahead of them. Kristi stood there for a moment, taking in the changes in Kyle. If anything, he looked more handsome. He'd put on some weight that he carried well. The laugh lines around his blue eyes and the lines around his mouth gave mute evidence

that the years in between had been happy ones
for him. She hugged him to her.

"You're looking great, Kyle. Sexier than
ever. I bet Francine has to beat all your admir-
ers off with a stick whenever you leave the
place."

He grinned as he tucked his arm around her
waist and headed her down the hallway to the
kitchen. "Not so you'd notice," he drawled.
"If you don't mind my saying so, you're looking awfully thin, seems to me."

"This isn't considered thin, I want you to
know." She paused for a moment and posed.
"This is all the rage in New York—willowy
and winsome." She blinked up at him with an
exaggerated pout. "Surely you've noticed."

"You might look great by New York stan-
dards, honey, but I'd say you look like you're
sickening over something. I've got newborn
calves that look healthier than you do." He
burst out laughing at her offended expression.
She gave up trying to look wounded and joined
him.

"It's been years since I heard you two trad-
ing insults, but you sound like you've had daily
practice," Francine commented as they sat

down at the table. "Nothing changes, regardless of the time passing."

But Kristi was aware that there had been changes. During the meal she enjoyed watching Francine and Kyle with their children. Pride and love for their offspring glowed in both faces. Kyle answered Kevin's perpetual stream of questions with no sign of impatience. Francine made sporadic conversation with Kristi while taking time to see that Kari got enough food on her plate.

Kyle glanced over and spoke to Francine. "Did you call Jase and tell him Kristi was here?"

Kristi's heart thudded to a halt. As it slowly picked up its rhythm once more, she waited for Francine's answer.

"No, as a matter of fact, I didn't think about it." She frowned slightly as she looked at her husband. "Do you think I should?"

Kristi realized that they were worried about Jason. Had she been so wrapped up in her own grief that she'd never given thought to his? She kept her eyes on her plate as she waited for Kyle's answer.

"It may not be necessary. He sent word earlier he might not make it. Said something about running late and if he wasn't here by six-thirty or so, not to expect him.'' Kristi glanced up to see her brother watching her. Silently she pleaded with him not to discuss Jason at the moment.

The conversation veered to other subjects, for which Kristi was thankful. She wondered if her brother knew how much Jason drank these days. She could hardly mention it to him, under the circumstances. Could his drinking habits have anything to do with her? Suddenly, she felt the need for reassurance that her absence in his life hadn't had such a debilitating effect on him. Jason was so strong. She had never pictured him as having any weaknesses. Could it be possible that he was vulnerable where she was concerned? She had a lot to think about before she would be ready to talk with Jason.

Kyle saddled one of the horses for Kristi after lunch and they spent the afternoon together. He showed her the many changes and improvements he had made, was making, or intended to make. It was obvious that he was content with his life and his family. He had all kinds of questions regarding her work, her life, and whether she was happy. The subject of

Jason was conspicuous by its absence from the conversation. Whatever his feelings regarding their split, Kyle obviously intended to stay out of it.

Kyle halted his horse at the edge of a small creek and stepped down from the saddle; then he helped Kristi down.

Although she'd kept up with her riding as often as possible while back East, she could already feel the sore muscles that complained she'd gone far enough today. *How quickly they forget,* she thought ruefully as she rubbed her tender bottom.

"How long are you going to be able to stay?" Kyle asked as he watched Kristi wander over to a grassy spot and gingerly lower herself to the ground.

"I don't have an assignment until the first of June, but I doubt I'll stay here that long."

"Why not?"

Nothing like being direct, dear brother, she thought with a twinge of exasperation. "That's rather a long time to visit anyone, don't you think? We're talking about two months or more."

Kyle threw himself down beside her in a lazy sprawl. "That depends. Do you think you'll be too bored to stay that long?"

"Of course not. I'm more afraid you'll be tired of having me around."

Kyle watched her for a few moments, enjoying having her home, wishing he could solve whatever her problems might be, but knowing that wasn't possible. It was her life—she needed to be in charge of her decisions. They were quiet for a while, savoring the peace of the afternoon, before Kyle sat up, peering at the hills in front of them. "Guess we'd better head back toward home. You're going to be feeling this little trip for a few days, I'm afraid."

"And here all the time I thought you were just being too polite to mention it." She groaned as she got up. "I should have known better than to think you'd ever be polite to me."

They mounted and started home at a slow pace, to help ease the strain on Kristi's unused muscles. All she could think about was soaking in a hot bath for hours. *Welcome home, Kristi,* she thought with wry humor. *We're going to have to get you toughened up, it seems.*

* * *

An exhausted Jason pulled into Kyle's yard late that afternoon. Everything that could possibly have gone wrong that day had managed to do so. They'd found a fence down, which meant unplanned hours of chasing cattle back through the break, and one of his men had received a nasty tear on his arm when some barbed wire suddenly snapped and wrapped around it. Plus, he'd been fighting the granddaddy of all hangovers most of the day.

And, worst of all, he'd been remembering the months after Kristi had left. He couldn't sleep then; he would lie awake night after night trying to come to terms with what had happened to their marriage. He'd made some really stupid mistakes with her. In his need to protect her from all unpleasantness he'd refused to explain what he was doing on the nights he was away from home. Once she left, it was too late.

He had discovered that he could sleep when he drank himself into oblivion, which he proceeded to do every night until Kyle finally stormed over one night and lit into Jason for trying to destroy himself. He had managed to pierce the apathy surrounding Jason and had made him so mad that he had taken a swing at Kyle, much to Kyle's delight. He'd provoked a reaction—as he had hoped to do.

Jason had stopped drinking and slowly learned to live with his ghosts. Until last night. What had happened to him last night?

He shook his head in disgust as he swung his truck around the house and came to an abrupt stop behind a fire-engine-red Triumph with New York license plates.

"Oh, my God!" He sat there staring at the car. Kristi. Of course it was Kristi. Somewhere deep inside he must have known it was her. How else could he explain his responses?

His thoughts flew back to the night before. Where earlier he'd ruthlessly shoved the upsetting memories away, now he searched for them frantically, wanting to relive each one.

It had worked! He'd lured her to Texas after he'd almost given up hope. A slow smile crept across his weary face. So she wanted a divorce, did she? No woman could respond to a man as Kristi had last night without having strong feelings for him.

Had she intended to go to bed with him? Somehow he didn't think so. She'd been too aloof until they danced together. Once again he felt her body pressed against his, moving languorously to the music.

Now that she was home, he'd move on to the next phase of his plan. Discovering that she hadn't been able to overcome her attraction to him gave him an edge he hadn't counted on. He certainly intended to use every advantage he could get. Kristi had belonged to him from the day her mother had first placed the tiny infant in his arms. He wasn't about to lose her now that he had her in his territory again.

A very subdued Kristi sat soaking in hot water. Although her muscles felt better, her conscience still smarted. She'd been looking at her actions of five years ago through the eyes of her family and Jason and didn't much like what she saw. Had she really been that selfish? Or had she just been immature? She'd discovered that several notions she'd hugged to herself for years needed to be tossed out the window.

Where did that leave her? The only thing she knew for certain was that, regardless of what she felt for Jason—and admittedly she was very confused about that—there was no way their marriage could work. She was another person now and they had nothing in common. Somehow she needed to convince him of that. If only he didn't have such a stronghold on her emotions.

Getting ready for supper, Kristi slipped into a cinnamon-colored caftan; its slim lines clung to her long legs. She tied her hair loosely in a topknot. She was stepping into heelless slippers when she heard Jason's voice. Surprised, she paused and unabashedly listened.

"Whose car is that outside, Francie? Looks a little out of place with the pickups and station wagons around here, don't you think?" His voice sounded pleasant, almost cheerful.

"Oh, hi, Jase." Francine's voice revealed her nervousness.

So Jason had come for supper after all, and no one had bothered to warn him that she was home. Feeling sorry for Francine, Kristi left her room. After all, she had the advantage. He had no idea she was around, nor did he know she was the woman he'd spent the night with. The thought amused her, at the same time she mentally acknowledged the butterflies that had suddenly taken up residence somewhere in her middle. She paused at the doorway of the kitchen, drinking in the sight of the man standing by the table. There were tired lines in his face, dark circles under his eyes. He looked like hell. But then, he didn't get much sleep last night.

That thought brought a slight smile to her face. "Hello, Jay-son."

He spun on his heel, taking her in at a glance. The look in his eyes caused Kristi to panic. He knew! Somehow he'd known that she was here and that he'd spent the night with her. His elevated brow even acknowledged the slight mimicry in her pronunciation of his name. Then she had no more time to think.

Jason moved with swift strides across the room and pulled her into his arms. Without a word he lowered his lips to hers. The kiss was a continuation of the ones they'd shared the previous evening. It spoke of wanting, of loving, of never-ending need, and effectively wiped out every coherent thought in Kristi's head. She clung to him, knowing that if he were to release her she'd fall in a heap at his feet. His kiss was leisurely and very thorough. Finally, he eased his hold and withdrew his lips enough to whisper, "Welcome home, Mrs. McAlister."

"Jase?"

He laughed, and his laughter was an unrestrained, joyous sound. Pulling her tightly against him once again, he murmured, "Good. At least you still recognize me. That's a start." He swung her around so they faced an astonished Francie. She was no more surprised than Kristi. Of all the ways Kristi might have envisioned their meeting, this one hadn't come to mind. Jason's eyes sparkled as he spoke to Francine. "I take it you intended to surprise me. You couldn't have given me a nicer one." He kept his arm securely wrapped around Kristi's waist, making it plain that he had no intention of releasing her any time soon.

"Well, not exactly, Jason," Francine stuttered, trying to get a grip on her thoughts. She'd never seen him like this before. Did he think Kristi had come home to him? Surely not. He was the one who'd told them about the divorce. Then what was going on? She hurried to explain. "I mean, we knew she was coming for a visit but she didn't say when, just some time in the next few weeks. Kyle said you might not make it over tonight, so I didn't think to call and tell you."

Kristi thought she knew Jason in all of his moods, but, like Francine, she couldn't decipher this one. She could feel the tenseness in his body, pressed so intimately against her side. She also knew that he'd been as affected by their kiss as she, but she couldn't understand why there wasn't some animosity or resentment toward her. After all, she had played a rather underhanded trick the night before by not identifying herself. Or had he known who she was all along?

Kyle bounded into the room from outside. "Glad you could make it, Jason. Sorry I'm late. I'll get washed up and we can sit down." He glanced at Jason's arm possessively wrapped around Kristi and smiled. Then he turned to Francine. "Where are the kids?"

"Oh, I fed them earlier. There was a special on television they wanted to watch, and I thought we could visit better without them."

Kristi took the respite and attempted to move away from Jason, a little surprised when he allowed it. She'd made a mistake in underestimating this man. She'd been feeling sorry for him and what she'd inadvertently done to him. She would need all of her wits about her to deal with this frankly sensual male whose eyes openly stripped her of everything she had painstakingly placed on her body. That was definitely an X-rated look he was giving her, and she wasn't unaffected by it.

The meal turned out to be much more pleasant than Kristi had imagined. She began to relax slightly as the four of them shared years of memories. It was as though each of them had made a pact to recall only the good times, and there had been many of them.

When Kyle started reminding them of some of the things that had happened because of Kristi's impulsiveness, and her red-hot temper, laughter rang out, including Kristi's. Yes, she could certainly understand what a handful she'd been for all of them.

Laughing as she raised her glass, Kristi looked at Jason's face and froze. For a moment he allowed her to see the overpowering love and need he felt for her, then he dropped his eyes, leaving her shaken.

Jason sat there soaking up Kristi's nearness as she visited with her family. Had she laughed last night, he would have known immediately who she was. He had always enjoyed her laughter. She hadn't had much to laugh about after they were married. If she gave him the chance, he would make sure their life together was happier. She *had* to give them another chance.

After the children were in bed, the four adults sat around in the living room. The men talked about ranching and the women listened. Feeling comfortably drowsy, Kristi was unprepared for Jason to stand up and say, ''Why don't you come home with me tonight, Kristi? We have some catching up to do.'' Her face flamed crimson. Then he added, ''We have quite a lot to talk about that really isn't of interest to Kyle and Francine.''

He'd done it on purpose! Her flush went even darker when she recognized that Kyle hadn't missed any of the byplay and was amused.

Kristi stood up and said coolly, ''No, thank you. I don't think that's a very good idea under the circumstances, Jason. Besides, I've got a lot of *catching up* to do—'' he smiled at her emphasis ''—with Kyle and Francine as well.''

He stalked catlike toward the door and paused. ''Then how about walking me to my truck?'' She caught the look Kyle and Francine exchanged and could have kicked him.

Why did he have to sound as though he could hardly wait to get his hands on her?

"All right," she agreed, determined to let him know exactly what she thought of his behavior. Neither one of them said anything until they reached his truck. The faint light from the porch bathed Jason's face in a golden glow as he looked at her car, then back at her.

"What was last night all about, Kristi? Is that the way divorces are taken care of in New York?"

She'd known it was coming and had decided that he wouldn't have it all his own way. "I didn't think you'd remember much about last night, Jason."

The hat Jason had put on as he stepped out of the house was shoved to the back of his head. "Very funny. The only thing I'm hazy about is why I woke up in your bed."

Dancing lights began to fill her eyes as a mischievous grin appeared on her face. "Probably because that's where you fell asleep—or passed out, whichever best describes your condition."

"Never mind my condition, what the hell were you trying to accomplish?"

"Would you believe nothing? I saw you go into the lounge and decided to let you know I was in town." She leaned against the truck in a deceptive pose of relaxation. Her nerves sang at his closeness. "I didn't know what to say when you didn't recognize me, so I decided not to say anything." She was glad he couldn't hear her heart beating a frantic rhythm in her breast.

He touched her cheek lightly with his palm, causing alarms to go off throughout her body. "What were you doing there, anyway?" His voice was husky, and he seemed to be more aware of her than of their conversation. She was having a little trouble concentrating herself.

"I'd decided to wait and get a good night's sleep before coming on to the ranch. I was on my way to dinner when I spotted you."

He leaned down and feathered light kisses along her jawline. "I didn't see you."

"No. You walked across the lobby like a man with a purpose which was one of the reasons I was surprised to find you alone."

"You had other reasons to be surprised?" His arms were now around her waist, forcing

her against his body so there was no way she
could ignore the effect she was having on him.

"The Jason McAlister I knew wouldn't have
sat in a bar for hours drinking alone. That
surprised me." She forced her eyes to meet his,
knowing that he could see her expression by
the porch light.

His hands roved caressingly along her sides,
stroking her. "Would you be interested in
sticking around to rehabilitate me?" He
paused, but she refused to answer. "People
change, Kristi. You have...I have...that's part
of life. But one thing has never changed...."

Her hands lay against his chest where she
felt the heavy thump of his heart. She was
drowning in the sensations he caused within
her. "What's that?" she managed to mumble.

"The way we react to each other." His
mouth came down on hers in a searing possession that robbed her of thought. Her mouth
parted, inviting his invasion, and his tongue
took advantage by slipping between her lips.
She felt the sigh he gave deep within his chest
and her body warmed to the nearness of him
as he pressed her back against the cab of the
truck. One of his hands found the zipper at her

throat and slid it down to her waist, giving him access to her breasts.

Kristi's arms slid around his lean torso, her hands insinuating themselves into his tight jeans and pulling the shirttail away so she could feel the hard muscles of his back as they rippled under her touch. How many times had she fantasized about holding him like this? She knew his body as well as her own and she quickly refamiliarized herself with the muscular feel of his shoulders, then the ridge of his spine.

His lips were making their own discoveries as they slid down her neck and explored the valley between her pink-tipped breasts. He could smell her light perfume—the perfume that had haunted him the night before—the teasing fragrance that had lingered with him all day.

Suddenly, Jason jerked away from Kristi and, with trembling hands, pulled her zipper up to its position under her chin. He buried his head in her neck, holding her achingly close to his aroused body. "Come home with me, Kristi," he murmured. "Let me love you."

Kristi clung to him, trying to regulate her breathing. She felt as though she'd been on a carnival ride too long, her head whirling. How could he continue to have this effect on her? She couldn't give in to her purely physical reaction to him, she just couldn't.

She shook her head. "I can't, Jase. Don't you see? It would solve nothing."

He grinned as he took long breaths like a runner after crossing the finish line. "I can think of one or two problems it would solve."

She moved away from him, needing the distance to get her emotions under control. Then she glanced back at him as he leaned against the truck, watching her. "I don't belong in Texas, Jase, surely you recognize that. My career is in New York. That's where I live—where I want to live. We should have ended our marriage years ago." He became very still, studying her like a hunter stalking his prey. "Why won't you sign the divorce papers?"

He jerked open the door and stepped into the cab of his truck. "I refuse to discuss it with you here. We can go home and go into it if you wish."

"Not tonight, Jason." She moved closer to the truck, and he suddenly reached out and caught her, pulling her to him. She didn't resist, feeling the power in his arm as it drew her closer to the window of the cab.

He nodded. "All right, not tonight," he agreed. "I'll give you some time with your family, then I'm coming to get you. You might as well accept it." He cupped his hand around the back of her head and brought her mouth down to his, touching her lips in a surprisingly soft kiss that ignored the passion pulling them together. "I'll never let you go, Kristi, you may as well understand that right now," he muttered as he released her.

She stood watching as he backed out and drove away, her fingertips pressed against her mouth, swollen from his possession. What had she done by coming back? She had been sure she could resist him, only to be proven wrong the first time she saw him again.

A very thoughtful Kristi returned to the house and her family.

Four

The next few days drifted through Kristi's life like a soft breeze whispering in the cotton-wood trees. She got acquainted with her niece and nephew, and reacquainted with Kyle and Francine. Unconsciously she waited for Jason to reappear.

One midafternoon found Kristi in the porch swing, reading one of the books she'd brought to catch up on. The wind rattled the leaves of the large cottonwoods planted nearby, blocking out the sound of a truck pulling into the yard. Engrossed in her book, she was startled to hear an unforgettable voice.

"Must be interesting reading."

Jason stood on the bottom step, one foot propped on the next step. Dusty Levi's gave evidence to his busy day. The color of his shirt came close to matching the sherry of his eyes as they stared at her through narrowed lids.

Kristi's gaze moved over him eagerly, and she realized how much she'd been looking forward to seeing him again. Not a good sign for her original plans. As his eyes lazily studied her, she nervously fingered the top button of her jade green shirt. She watched him as he sauntered toward her with his silent stride.

Several different swings had decorated the porch over the years, but none had seemed so small as this one when Jason settled into the space beside her. The spicy fragrance of his after-shave mingled with the scent of his warm body, and Kristi had to struggle to control her own body's reaction to him.

He dropped his arm along the back of the swing. "Where is everyone?"

Kristi reached for her single braid nervously, needing to keep her hands occupied as she absently pulled on it. "Francine took the kids into town. I decided to stay home and read.'' She twisted the braid around her hand. ''I'm not sure where Kyle is.''

Jason gently removed the plait from her twisting fingers and stroked it. Trying to ignore her response to his presence, she unwisely burst into speech. ''What do you want?'' The minute the words left her mouth she knew she'd said the wrong thing. She watched the smile appear on his face with fatalistic calm, but he surprised her by letting the provocative question pass.

''I wondered if you'd like to go with me this afternoon. You used to enjoy riding with me and I need to check out the river section.'' He continued to play with her braid as he talked. The message in Jason's eyes was about another subject. Her mind flashed to their night together and how good they had been with each other. His eyes registered similar thoughts. He lightly brushed the soft curls that clung to her neck as he waited for her answer.

A light shiver ran through her at his touch. Was he aware of the effect he had on her?

When she didn't answer him, he continued. ''One of the men reported seeing smoke in the south part of my property a few days ago. I need to take a ride and check it out; we've found people camping there in the past." He grinned as his hand slid around the nape of her neck. "My property is a little too easy to reach from the other side of the river."

Kristi knew of the narrowness of the Rio Grande along this area. During the dry summer months there were times when it dried up enough so that people could walk across without difficulty.

"Are you having trouble with illegal aliens?" she asked in an attempt to show him how little effect he had on her. She wasn't sure whether she succeeded. Jason knew her too well.

He began to massage the taut muscles in her neck. "You could say that." He nodded, a little amused at her serious expression.

"Kyle mentioned something the other night, but said there hasn't been much publicity in order not to discourage the tourists from visiting Mexico." She shifted slightly, hoping to move away from his body, but there wasn't enough room in the swing.

"I know, but I don't agree with the theory. I don't think the tourists have any business going into the interior right now."

"What's happening?"

"Mexico's poor economy has created an internal turmoil that's become explosive. The peso's been devalued twice in the past five years. Those who can, sneak across the river to find work." His face settled into grim lines. "Not that I blame them, but the Naturalization authorities watch all of us here on the border, trying to insure that we don't hire any of them. I can't afford to have them camping on my land." He grinned. "I don't expect to find anyone today, though." He tilted her chin so she was looking up at him. "Do you want to come?"

When he looked at her like that, she found him impossible to resist. "I might as well." She glanced down at the forgotten book in her hand. She had no idea what it was about. "I'll need to change shoes," she said as she stood up, more to get away from Jason's seductive presence than because she was in a hurry to leave.

He followed her into the house, which did nothing for Kristi's peace of mind. Hoping to deter him, she murmured, "I'll be right back." She discovered when she came out of her closet with an old pair of riding boots that she hadn't stopped him. He stood in the middle of the bedroom, looking around at the furnishings and at her personal belongings scattered around the room. "I never said I was neat," she muttered as she sat down on the bed to pull off her sandals.

"That's true, you never did," he agreed with a grin. His gaze traveled leisurely across her body, causing it to tingle as though he'd actually touched her. "However, you do have other redeeming virtues."

She refused to allow him to see how his teasing affected her. With admirable nonchalance she stood up, stamping her feet into the boots. "That's true. Just consider me the drinking cowboy's gift, come to console you in your time of need." She glanced at him from beneath thick lashes. "You never did tell me why you needed consoling the other night."

"Can't remember. Your consoling did the trick." They stood there in the bedroom, both conscious of the bed a couple of feet away. She would give a great deal to know what he remembered of that night. Was he aware how much she gave of herself, or that she'd never been with anyone else?

"Will I need a jacket?"

"It wouldn't hurt. I'm not sure how long we'll be. You might want to leave a message for the Coles."

Kristi left a note on the kitchen table, propped against the squat sugar bowl. She had a strong hunch that neither Kyle nor Francine would be surprised to learn she'd gone with Jason.

Kristi noticed the changes Jason had made to the property as they drove up to the ranch headquarters. The most noticeable was the blacktop on the formerly graveled road, an improvement which greatly reduced the dust in the area. The large two-story frame house had a fresh coat of white paint with a bright blue trim that lent a pleasing decorative touch. The familiar giant live oak trees continued to cast their generous shade around the house, framing it protectively.

Jason parked the truck and started for the barn. Kristi followed more slowly as she silently registered the well-kept appearance of the place. She glanced toward the house and wondered if Molly still worked for him.

As she watched Jason saddle two of his horses, she asked about Nate and Molly.

"Oh, yes. I doubt that I could function around here without those two. Molly still tries to fatten me up and Nate makes sure I don't get too complacent by pointing out the mistakes I make." His warm tones, more than his words, expressed his feelings for the couple.

Jason led the horses toward the house. "I need to pick up something—come in and say hello to Molly." His arm came around her in a familiar gesture and rested on her shoulders. He gave a gentle tug and settled her against his lean body as they followed the path to the house.

Molly greeted Kristi with a hug and beaming smile. "With that pigtail hanging over your shoulder, you barely look sixteen." She paused, taking in Kristi's slim build. "Actually, you were more curvy back then than you are now."

Jason burst out laughing at the expression on Kristi's face. When she glared at him he spread his hands in a gesture of innocence. "What can I say, Kristi? Molly's always been one to tell it like it is." He paused, his gaze touching her body like a caress as he drawled, "What did you do with those curves, anyway?"

He prevented Kristi's swing from connecting with his shoulder by grasping her wrist. His maneuver didn't improve her temper, nor did her obvious irritation prevent his laughter.

Turning to Molly, Jason mentioned that he was taking Kristi with him. He reached into the refrigerator and took out a large container which he slipped into a sack.

"Oh, before I forget, Jase. Mr. Alvarez called."

Jason looked up sharply. "When?"

"Must have been about half an hour ago. He left a number." She handed him a slip of paper.

Jason stood there for a moment, his head down, then he seemed to come to a decision. "Excuse me." He smiled at Kristi. "I'd better get back to him." He walked through the door leading to the hall and his office.

Kristi looked around the room. Changes had been made inside as well. "The place looks great, Molly. Jason's made quite a few improvements." Her gaze fell on the microwave.

Molly smiled. "That he has. Something set him off a few months ago. He had a crew in doing some remodeling inside and refurbishing out."

"What sort of remodeling?"

"Oh, he knocked out a wall upstairs and enlarged the master bedroom, added a nice large bathroom off of it, all fancy and modern. Kinda surprised me—he's in the house so seldom."

A few months ago, Kristi thought. She'd first contacted him about the divorce a few months ago. Why would that have anything to do with his making changes in the house? Did he remember her once mentioning how nice it would be to have another bathroom? If he'd signed the papers she would have assumed that he was planning to remarry, but he'd been adamantly against the divorce.

They needed to discuss their relationship. Their lives had gone in different directions over the past five years. They could no longer ignore the situation.

Jason's voice exploded from his office, interrupting her reverie. "Come off it, Alvarez. I waited in town for hours the other night and you canceled on me. Dammit, man, you know I've got to have your help. We can't waste any more time."

Molly and Kristi glanced at each other, then away, embarrassed to have heard his private conversation. When Jason rejoined them, he looked dangerous. Kristi decided she wouldn't want to be the one who crossed him.

He picked up the package he had taken from the refrigerator and started toward the door. "I'll see you later, Molly." When he reached the horses, he began to fill a saddlebag with the contents of his sack. It looked like food. Surely they weren't going to be gone long enough to eat, although she knew from experience that Jason never left the ranch headquarters without some supplies, including water and his battered coffeepot.

As they rode toward the southern rolling hills, Kristi enjoyed the day's promise of springtime. It was her favorite time of year in Texas. In another couple of months it would be so hot that going without a hat would guarantee sunstroke. Now she let her hat sit on the back of her head as she renewed her acquaintance with Jason's heritage.

"Do you ever think about living somewhere else, Jase?"

He'd been deep in thought and her question pulled him away from whatever caused his brow to crease so deeply. He, too, scanned the wide open area before them. He shook his head. "My time in the service convinced me that I wouldn't be happy anywhere else. Why?"

"I just wondered. I can't even picture you in any other surroundings."

They rode along in silence, Kristi concentrating on the scenery around them as she remembered her first days and nights in New York, miserably homesick, yet refusing to consider returning home.

The rolling hills were deceptive, looking smooth until they moved closer to view the rough ground, scraggly mesquite trees and occasional cactus. Clumps of grass grew in sparse oases of green and Kristi noticed several dry creek beds. The weather had not been kind to the area in recent months.

Jason eventually reined in and stepped out of the saddle, checking the ground. Kristi put gentle pressure on the bit as her horse also came to a stop. Remains of a large campfire were in evidence, but whoever had built it had taken into consideration the dry conditions. Large stones had been placed in a tight ring around the blackened dirt, which sat in an open clearing. As she signaled her horse forward, Kristi noted that the creek bed here was larger, fed by an underground spring that bubbled nearby. The area was peaceful and she had trouble seeing it as a possible spot for conflict.

Kristi eased from the saddle with care and ambled over to the side of the creek. A couple of weeping willow trees leaned close to the side, as though embracing the life-giving liquid rippling by. Glancing south, she wondered how far they were from the Rio Grande and how many people had gathered around a warm fire at this spot on the first night of what they hoped would be a new life.

She glanced over her shoulder then spun around and demanded, "What are you doing?"

"What's it look like I'm doing?" Jason replied as he continued his task.

"It looks like you're unsaddling our horses," she responded in a testy tone.

Jason solemnly acknowledged her comment. "Give the little lady a prize for being observant." Without looking in her direction he pulled off bedrolls from the saddles and unrolled them near the stone-ringed fire pit. "Why don't you look around for some wood—we might as well have a hot meal."

"Jason! We can't spend the night out here!"

"Why not?" he asked, stopping what he was doing and gazing at her with a steady look, his hands resting lightly on his hips.

"You know very well why not. Francine and Kyle will wonder what happened to me."

"Why should they? You left them a note saying you'd be with me." He began to pull packages out of the saddlebags and place them on the stones.

"They won't be expecting me to spend the night and you know it." Impatiently she watched him settling in. "What's this all about, anyway?"

"I wondered when you might think to ask that question." He reached into his pocket and pulled out a battered pack of cigarettes. Then he took one and stuck it between his lips. Cupping a lit match, he touched it to the end of the cigarette, inhaled, then blew out the match.

Kristi was no longer the wide-eyed eighteen-year-old who accepted each pearl of wisdom from his lips without question. Unfortunately, at twenty-four she still had to fight her strong feelings for him, despite his arrogance.

"If I'd known we were playing games I'd have asked for the rule book," she commented sweetly.

Her answer was not what he expected. In fact, her attitude was different from anything he'd seen in her, and he knew her well, or so he thought. His eyes narrowed as he took in her belligerent stance, then he began to smile. He may have married a girl, but he had a full-size woman on his hands now. He needed to remember that. "Relax, Kristi. I thought it would be a good idea for us to get away and give ourselves a chance to get reacquainted. You used to enjoy camping out—I thought you might like it now." He paused, drawing on his cigarette. "Do you really think Kyle and Francine are going to expect me to return you to them tonight?"

The blaze of desire that lit his eyes scorched Kristi across the space between them. The slanting sun cast shadows across the campsite and Kristi dropped her eyes, no longer able to meet his gaze.

Unable to find an answer for him, she remembered his earlier comment. "I'll look for firewood," she muttered as she looked around. Since the same thought must have been in the minds of the previous visitors, the immediate vicinity was bare of anything burnable.

Glancing across the creek, she decided to start hunting over there.

Jason watched her graceful movements as she crossed the creek, stepping on the stones uncovered by the gurgling water. He wondered if he would get his fill of just looking at her. After enduring the past few years, he rather doubted it.

He started after her.

They found several low-growing bushes and a few dead branches broken off mesquite trees. The companionable search relaxed Kristi as it brought back memories of earlier times. Jason had been right. She'd always enjoyed camping, and he and Kyle and Francine had often spent as long as a week out together when she was growing up. Had those times meant as much to Jason as they had to her?

By the time they returned to camp and got the fire going, it was dark. The smell of the burning mesquite erased the years as they cooked their meal. Jason's mysterious packages had contained ground beef hash, reheated pinto beans and cornbread ready to be baked in an iron skillet. After eating a heaping plate of the familiar fare, Kristi felt that she was truly back in Texas.

The bedrolls were placed end to end by the fire and Kristi leaned back on hers and studied the night sky. She'd forgotten how bright the stars looked away from the night glow of the city. She could feel the tension seep from her as she gave herself up to the night and her surroundings. For this time, at least, she could pretend there'd been no years in between. She moved her head lazily to watch Jason as he stirred the campfire, adding more wood. He placed the coffeepot over the fire and the aroma of fresh coffee wafted to her, teasing her senses. Coffee always seemed to taste better when made over an open fire, as though it absorbed the wood smoke as well.

Jason settled back on his bedroll with a contented sigh and admired the long length of Kristi stretched out so relaxed nearby.

"I've missed you, Kristi."

His husky voice reverberated through her body. Warm green eyes reflected the firelight as she watched him.

"I've missed you, too, Jase."

"Then why didn't you come home?"

"I couldn't."

He made an impatient move, then stopped abruptly. Slowly lighting another cigarette, he asked, "Why not?"

She gazed into the fire for a long moment before attempting an answer. "I couldn't face you, knowing I'd failed as a wife. I had to gather strength by looking forward until I was strong enough to look back."

The night sounds around them were a muted background to their low voices. The fire crackled occasionally, sending its sparks toward the bright stars flickering overhead. The faint call of a coyote drifted toward them and Kristi shivered at the lonely sound.

Jason's voice was low when he finally spoke. "I never realized you felt that you'd failed as my wife." She could hear pain in his voice, which surprised her. "I wish I'd known, so I could have reassured you." He'd been staring into the fire but with his last remark he turned his head, and his pain was reflected on his face. "I'm sorry I didn't understand before. Why did you feel you had failed?"

His question brought painful memories flooding through her and she slid her arms around her bent knees and squeezed, trying to control her feelings. "Because I couldn't have the family you wanted...because you were gone so much...because you had a life away from me that you wouldn't share." She forced herself to meet his gaze as she attempted a smile. "I was such a child in so many ways. I didn't know what you expected of me, and I failed at the only thing I could do to make you want me."

Her obvious pain thrust into him like a knife blade and without thinking he moved over toward her. His shadow blanketed her for a moment, as he stood between her and the fire. For the first time she felt the chill of the night air. Then he settled beside her and pulled her into his arms as though he could erase the anguish she was feeling.

"Hush, Kristi, love. You don't know what you're talking about. You're all I've ever wanted...everything that I could possibly want, and you've always been that for me. I thought you knew."

She shook her head mutely against his shoulder as he held her against him.

"You must understand that you were more than a baby machine to me. Besides, you never gave us a chance to be parents after that. The doctor said we should wait a few months before even attempting another pregnancy." He paused. He shook her gently. "Remember?"

She nodded her head, but refused to look at him. He lowered them both so they were stretched full-length on her bedroll. It felt so good to have her back in his arms. For a while Jason was content to lie there with her snuggled against him. The conversation brought back many painful memories for him. How differently he might have handled her if he'd understood her insecurities.

"I wish I'd been more open with you about what I was doing back then."

His remark caused Kristi to pull away and stare up at him in surprise. Although those mysterious trips played a major part in her nightmares during that time in her life, she never expected to receive an explanation. She wondered why he mentioned them now.

"I had some cockeyed idea that I was protecting you from the harsh realities of life. Instead, I caused you to face different ones that weren't even necessary." His eyes full of love, he traced an invisible line along her jaw with his forefinger.

Kristi watched the shadows cast by the flickering firelight with fascination as they highlighted Jason's serious face. *How can I possibly cut this man out of my life,* she thought with quiet despair, *when he's part of me.*

Jason stared into the fire as he began to talk. "I was with the Army intelligence unit when I was in the service. When I got out, I did my best to forget that part of my life, but things don't always work out the way you want them to." His hand moved down her neck in a gentle stroking movement. Kristi caught her breath at the immediate response of her body to his touch. She forced herself to concentrate on his words. "A couple of years after I returned home I was contacted by the government to help with a covert investigation along the border. Both governments were trying to put a stop to heroin smuggling between the two nations."

Kristi relaxed as Jason's hands worked their magic. His gaze had dropped to her once more and he leaned over and kissed her lightly on the lips. With a rueful shrug, he acknowledged, "Since my ranch is located on the border, it made sense that I could move back and forth without arousing suspicion."

Unexplained happenings took on new meaning as Kristi recalled the early days of her marriage. Would it have made a difference if she'd been aware of his activities at that time? She would never know now.

"Are you still involved with them?" Her tone reflected her relaxed state.

"No, I'm not." Jason's hand paused at the top button of her shirt, toyed with it for a moment, then slipped it loose. "We were able to get enough evidence against the ringleaders to bring them in about six months after you left." His hand moved to the next button. "By then it was too late for me to explain to you what I'd been doing." With the last button undone, Jason slid his hand back to the front opening of her bra and undid the hasp. "You seemed to be happy with your new life."

"What gave you that idea?" Her heart was beating so rapidly it shook her body.

"That's the impression you gave Francine whenever she talked with you."

"Why didn't you ever call me, Jase?" she asked in a breathless whisper.

"Because I knew better. If I'd heard your voice, I would've been on the next plane to

New York to drag you back home." His ragged tone did nothing for her peace of mind.

Her hand caressed the nape of his neck, feeling the springy hair that grew there, lost in the feeling of his lean strength pressed against her. "If that's the way you felt, why did you let me leave?"

His head bent toward her. "I had to face the fact that when I married you, you were too young to decide what you wanted in life." His hand cupped her breast, his fingers rubbing lightly over the peak until Kristi could no longer lie still. She shifted restlessly as his fingers edged to her other breast. "I'm not man enough to let you leave me like that again, Kristi, I'm sorry." Jason placed his lips with gentle care on hers, moving them in a silken glide that sent quivers rocketing down her body. As her lips softened in response, he moved his arms around her, drawing her closer to his hard frame.

Kristi responded to his possession, her tongue darting to meet his. He shifted his weight, lifted her and removed her blouse. Then he began to explore the soft contours of her body, the smooth silkiness of her back. He unsnapped her jeans and his hands followed the rounded contours of her hips as he slipped the rest of her clothes from her trembling body.

Had Jason said anything, whether imploring or demanding, perhaps Kristi could have resisted him. Instead, his silent seeking into her most secret places caused her to lose all desire to resist. She would enjoy this for just a while longer, then she must put a stop to it. She needed to explain to him there was no going back to their old relationship—they were two different people now—yet the feelings she was experiencing were familiar and very powerful.

Kristi wasn't aware when the lazy, exploring strokes changed to determined movements with definite goals. All she knew was that her body had burst into glorious flame wherever he touched. She moved closer to him, her hands searching his body. Her trembling fingers fumbled at the snaps of his shirt, hastily pulling until his chest was bared. Her hands explored the broad expanse of hard muscle and soft curls, relearning a once-familiar terrain. As her hands crept around his back, he shrugged off his shirt, then pulled her back to him. Her breasts pressed against him and she felt the quick catch of his breath at the touch.

Kristi's hands paused at his waist, frustrated in their attempts to renew her acquaintance with his body. She felt cool air play across her hot skin and realized that Jason had pulled away. Her eyelids fluttered open and she watched as he pulled off his boots and Levi's. She'd forgotten the strength in his hard muscled buttocks and thighs, the powerful body kept in whipcord condition.

He lay back down beside her, his legs tangling with hers, his arousal hard against her bare thigh. Kristi trembled with the force of her emotions. His hands drew a pattern on her inner thighs that sought to drive her out of her mind. Just as she thought he would stroke the most sensitive area, his hand would dance lightly away, only to begin the pattern once again.

"Oh, Jase," she moaned, wanting him to take her so badly she ached.

"I'm right here, honey."

"Love me, Jase. Oh, please, love me."

His uneven breathing tickled her ear and she knew how badly he wanted her, but he seemed intent on teasing them both by postponing their joining.

Her hand reached out and touched him as he nestled along her thigh. His whole body jerked at her touch. She stroked him, the full, strong length of him, and heard his groan. He raised himself, slipped his hands under her hips and pulled her up to him. Then he eased himself into the loving warmth of her body.

For long moments they lay there, held tightly in the closest embrace possible, his warmth filling her, her warmth surrounding him. When he began to move she wrapped her legs around him in an effort to absorb all of him. Her movement spurred him into a faster rhythm that caused Kristi to explode inside. He paused, holding her close until her body slowed the trembling from within, then he began to move once more.

Kristi was unfamiliar with the pleasure of reaching the peak of sexual gratification, then continuing. Her body seemed to be so much more sensitive to the sensations he created within her and it reacted to the stimulus with added fervency.

As Jason's rhythm increased once more, Kristi gripped him with such intensity that Jason had trouble breathing. Her pulsing body was more than he could withstand and he gave one final lunge into the deep softness that surrounded him. He was positive he'd felt the earth shake. Their ardent lovemaking served to sedate them and both fell asleep as they lay, in a tangle of arms, and legs on top of Kristi's bedroll.

As the night breeze grew more brisk, Jason stirred, moving carefully so he wouldn't wake the sleeping woman by his side. Stepping cautiously around the fire he grabbed his bedroll and unzipped it, moving it next to hers. He shifted Kristi into the opened bedroll, holding her close for a moment. Then, taking hers, he zipped the two together and pulled it over them. He pulled Kristi back into his arms, and she shifted until her head curved into the hollow of his shoulder.

He lay there for a long time, holding her in his arms as he stared at the silent stars blinking in the black night, before drifting off to sleep once more.

Five

Jason watched as morning light silhouetted the eastern hills. Kristi still slept soundly in the circle of his arms. How many nights had he dreamed that he held her in his arms, only to wake up alone? She had listened to him last night, but he wasn't sure how she felt. Her lovemaking had been spontaneous and fervent and he knew he still had the ability to arouse her, but did she still love him? Was she willing to make something of their marriage? He had loved her enough to let her go once before, but he knew he didn't have the strength to do it again. This was one contest he had to win in order to survive.

Kristi dreamed that Jason held her in his arms, his hands molding her to his body. She shifted closer to him, wanting to feel the power of his love once more, when she realized that she wasn't dreaming. Just as her eyes struggled open, his mouth found hers in a hotly passionate kiss and she melted into the arms already holding her.

His lovemaking that morning was aggressive and demanding—as though he couldn't get enough of her. The raging storm within him quickly ignited Kristi and she responded almost savagely. Tenderness had given way to raw passion and Kristi matched Jason's demands with equal fervor. She stayed with him this time and waited until she heard his cry as he went over the edge before she gave in to the sensations she'd fought to delay.

They lay gasping for air, damp from their exertions, their down-filled cover long since discarded. As she lay limply against him, Kristi felt Jason's chuckle start deep in his chest.

"You're something of a tiger when aroused, aren't you, lady?"

She thought about that for a moment, trying to equate the picture with her ice princess image. She began to smile as she reached up and smoothed the damp hair from his forehead. "Would you have preferred me to cringe and pull away?"

This time his laugh rumbled into the open. "You would have had a hell of a time trying to pull away this morning, that's for sure."

"That's what I decided," she answered demurely.

He shook his head in bewilderment. He didn't know this bewitching creature with the ability to tease when he least expected it. His love for Kristi had been with him for so long it was as essential to him as the air he breathed, but discovering the mature personality kept him slightly off-balance. He had a hunch she preferred him that way.

Kristi rested against him, admitted to herself that she felt as though she'd come home. All of her calm, rational plans to return to Texas and get Jason's signature on the divorce papers seemed to have drifted away in the smoke of their campfire the night before.

She sat up, ignoring the morning chill and her bareness. "Jason, we need to talk."

He watched the morning light touch the dainty curve of her breasts. He leaned over and kissed one of them lingeringly. "What about?"

"The divorce."

He stiffened, then slowly straightened to look at her. In a low, firm voice, he stated, "There will be no divorce, Kristi."

The chill Kristi felt was not entirely due to the morning breeze. He had misunderstood her. She tried to explain. "What I mean is—"

"I know what you mean, Kristi, and I'm telling you right now I don't intend to agree to it."

Frustrated that he wouldn't let her finish, she jumped up and looked around for her clothes. They lay near the bedroll on a clump of grass, for which she gave thanks. Sand would not improve them at all. She tried once more. "Would you just listen to me for a moment? I know how you feel—you've made that clear enough. It's just that my job is in New York and—"

"I know where your job is, damn it. I've known for five lousy years." Jason had grabbed his clothes and was dressed by the time he finished speaking. He filled the coffeepot with water and set it to the side as he began to rebuild the fire. "I thought from your response to me you were willing to consider staying here. Obviously, I was wrong."

Determined not to lose her temper, she waited until her voice sounded calm. "It isn't quite that simple, Jason. I have certain commitments—"

"You sure as hell do. You made a commitment to me before you decided modeling was your lifelong dream. That's a commitment you've been willing to overlook until now."

"That's not true, Jason, and you know it. I didn't think you wanted me. You didn't ask me to stay—you never called or wrote and asked me to come home. How was I to know you still wanted me?" She slid her hands in her back pockets as she glared at him.

The fire caught and Jason added the small twigs needed, then slowly stood up. "You should have known I still wanted you because I stand behind my commitments."

"To the bitter end. Yes, I know. Well, I didn't want to continue as your wife just because you were stuck with me. You wanted children—we both knew that—"

"Not that again. Yes, I wanted children, Kristi, but if you can't have them, then we won't have them. You're too important to me to give you up over an issue like that!" He stood a few feet away, glaring right back at her.

"I am?" Her voice faltered.

If anything, his frown deepened. "You're damned right."

"So why didn't you ever tell me?" she asked wistfully.

He threw up his hands in disgust. "I give up." He spun around and stalked away from the campsite.

Kristi wandered toward the stream, then crossed it as she sought some privacy among the brushy hills. She needed time to think.

Had she expected too much of Jason? He'd never been one to talk about his feelings, but she had always known he was there when she needed him. Maybe that was it. She had relied on him all her life without question, until they lost the baby, when she'd begun to question everything. Because he hadn't supplied the answers, she'd felt that he let her down.

What had she done to him?

When she returned to the campsite, Kristi caught the strong aroma of coffee brewing over the campfire. Jason sat near the fire and, when he saw her, grabbed the pot and poured two steaming cups full, setting one down beside him and blowing on the other. She murmured a soft "thanks" and picked up the cup, wrapping her fingers around it. She could feel his tension but was unsure what she could say that would ease it. Everything had seemed so clear before she arrived. Now their situation seemed like a tangled mass of thread, and she wasn't sure how to start unraveling the misunderstandings. In her youthful exuberance Kristi had thought that loving each other was all that was necessary to make a relationship work. She had learned painfully that, although vital, love wasn't enough. No relationship could survive unless the individuals involved communicated with each other and unless each had a basic understanding of the other's feelings.

She vented her frustration with a sigh.

"I want to ride down to the river," Jason announced. He stood up, reached for the saddlebags and brought out a wrapped package of cinnamon rolls. "You'd better eat something. Molly made these yesterday."

Kristi's mouth watered, remembering the taste from years past. She took one from him and bit into it, savoring the sharp bite of cinnamon and the creamy texture of icing. Glancing up, she noticed a slight smile curve the corner of Jason's mouth. Swallowing the bite, she asked, "What's so funny?"

He continued to take in the picture she made—her clothes wrinkled, her long braid matted and unkempt, her face shiny—then explained. "If your New York friends could only see you now."

She shrugged, unconcerned, and took another bite. New York seemed light-years away—an alien planet that had little allure.

After filling both cups with the remaining coffee, Jason packed the remaining items with sure, deft movements. He had both horses saddled and ready by the time Kristi finished her roll and coffee.

The day promised to be another warm one, with only a slight breeze. Jason seemed preoccupied as he followed a trail indiscernible to Kristi. They came over a rise and halted, and she was surprised to discover the river so close to their camping site. The Rio Grande flowed sluggishly by, looking muddy and ugly, hardly what would be expected of a major boundary between two nations. Kristi compared the two sides of the river and saw no difference. It was hard to believe that another government, another language, another way of life took over once the river was crossed.

Jason signaled his mount to move down the incline until he reached the banks of the river, then he rode along studying the ground. Eventually he angled away from the river once more and turned north. Kristi moved up alongside of him and glanced at his grim expression. Whatever he'd discovered, he didn't like it.

They rode for miles in silence, Kristi soon losing herself in thought. Jason had made his position clear. Where did that leave them? Her career required that she live in New York. Did she want to return to that busy world and continue as she had been during these last few years? Married, but not married? Is that what Jason wanted? What *did* he want?

The memory of his recent lovemaking brought a flush to her cheeks. He'd made it quite clear what he wanted! Could the magnetic force that pulled them together in such heated response to each other be a strong enough foundation for their relationship? Kristi glanced at Jason from the corner of her eye. His eyes searched the underbrush. He seemed unaware of her presence.

Kristi smiled as memories of other overnight camping trips came to mind—especially the ones they'd taken after their marriage. Had he always looked at her with such possession, as though branding her with every look? If Jason had his way, she would stay right there on the ranch with him, as he had intended when he married her.

I wonder what Jonathan would do if I were suddenly to call and tell him I want to retire? Would she miss the frenetic atmosphere, the excitement, the clothes, the money, the recognition?

She didn't know. She'd never considered it before.

They were little more than a mile away from the house when a horse and rider raced toward them, raising a cloud of dust that trailed behind like exhaust. It was one of Jason's ranch hands. He began to shout as he pulled up in front of them.

"Nate's been hurt, Mac," he panted. "We're afraid it's bad. No one knew where you were." He stopped to get his breath. "Molly had us bring him into the house and we called the doc, but he isn't here yet."

"How bad is he, Pete? What happened?" Jason's questions flew over his shoulder as he leaned over the long neck of his horse and took the lead. As they galloped, Kristi heard Pete answer.

"That new horse you bought started bounding around and threw him. Before we could get to him, the damned fool thing stepped on his leg. We heard the bone pop clear across the corral." They reached the yard and Jason leaped from his horse. "He may have some busted ribs, too. Molly's afraid he's got a concussion." Pete ran to keep up with Jason. "He don't look too good."

The string of expletives coming from Jason painted the air blue as he took the porch steps three at a time and disappeared into the house. Kristi had grabbed his horse's reins and led it down to the barn, knowing both animals needed cooling off.

Pete took the reins from her as she climbed down from the saddle. "I'll see to the horses, ma'am. You might want to go in to comfort Molly.''

Of course. Nate and Molly were inseparable. Kristi thought of them more as an institution than as a couple. She trotted back to the house.

As she passed Jason's office she heard him on the phone giving directions. He slammed down the receiver and strode past her down the hall. His voice sounded calm, as though he hadn't been giving orders and directions like a machine gun spitting out bullets.

"A helicopter will be here within fifteen minutes. They'll fly you to San Antone, Nate. You're going to be fine.''

Kristi paused at the door of one of the bedrooms and took in the tableau before her. Nate lay stretched out on top of the multicolored quilt covering the four-poster bed, his face as gray as his grizzled hair. Molly sat in a straight-backed chair by the bed, holding Nate's hand, appearing composed; but the panic in her eyes told of her real state. Jason stood at the end of the bed, legs braced, his hat still grasped in one hand, forgotten.

Nate had taken the place of Jason's father in his life. Jason fought to hang on to his control. Why the hell did these things have to happen?

Jason's glance fell on Molly. "You better get a bag packed, Molly. No tellin' how long you'll be in San Antone."

Molly looked up, startled. "I can't go with him, Jase. You've got those extra men coming in tomorrow to help with the inoculations and branding." Her eyes fell to the pasty face on the pillow, then looked up at Jason, trying to hide the welling tears.

Without glancing at Kristi, Jason replied brusquely, "Your place is with Nate, Molly. Don't worry. Kristi's here. She can handle this end."

Nate was the only one who didn't react to his statement. Molly's face broke into a trembling smile that would have lit a dark room, and Kristi's astonishment at being volunteered so casually would have been comical if the occasion hadn't been so serious.

"Oh, Kristi, could you?" Molly's voice quavered and she paused. "They'll only be here three days—but that's twelve hungry men to cook for."

The sardonic smile on Jason's face spurred Kristi's response. "Molly, there's no way I

could ever take your place, but I'll do my best
to see that none of them starve.'' She met Jason's amused gaze with a level one of her own.

The whumping sound of giant blades cutting through air grew louder and Molly
jumped up. "Oh, the helicopter's coming. I'll
be ready in just a moment.'' She dashed out of
the room faster than Kristi had ever seen her
move before.

Jason stepped over to Nate's side and
checked his pulse. Kristi heard a commotion
on the porch and stepped back into the hallway. She saw two paramedics with a stretcher
and bag push through the front door, and she
motioned to them.

A flurry of activity accompanied Nate's re-
moval from the house. Molly stayed as close to
Nate as possible as they carried him through
the kitchen and out to the waiting copter.
Kristi admired the well-planned procedure that
enabled the men to respond so quickly to
emergencies. As she followed them out the
door she saw Jason talking to the pilot.

A car slammed to a stop and the local doctor leapt out of it. Jason met him before he got
halfway to the house, but the noise from the
helicopter drowned out his explanations. Both

men stopped talking and watched as the large chopper lifted off and rapidly disappeared from sight. The strain on Jason's face was more evident now that his stoic attitude wasn't necessary.

"Hello, Dr. Johnson. It's good to see you, even if your trip out here was wasted." Kristi joined the two men, her memory relentlessly returning to the morning that this man had sat by the side of her bed attempting to comfort her.

"Kristi! I hadn't heard you were back, child. It's good to see you." He grabbed her hand and squeezed it affectionately while Jason watched them in silence.

"Do you have time for something to drink, Doctor?" she asked, pleased to see him again.

"I think I'll take time, Kristi. I'm just sorry I didn't get here sooner." He turned to the younger man. "What do you think, Jason? How bad was he?"

Jason rotated his shoulders in a weary gesture and turned toward the house, motioning Kristi and Dr. Johnson to go in front. "It's hard to tell, doc. The paramedics seemed to think he was in pretty good shape, from all his vital signs. We'll have to wait until Molly calls to find out what the X-rays show.''

Kristi was astonished to discover that it was after one o'clock when they reached the kitchen. *Jason must be hungry by now.* She checked the contents of the large refrigerator and smiled. They certainly wouldn't starve to death, that was certain. A large bowl of crisp vegetables waited, as well as slices of ham and roast beef. Potato salad nestled among pickled beets. Kristi began to set the food on the table, grabbing a pitcher of iced tea as she swung the refrigerator door shut.

It didn't take much convincing to get the doctor to stay and eat with them. After lunch Jason saw him off and returned to the kitchen, where he poured himself another cup of coffee. Kristi watched him, reminded again how seldom he showed what he was feeling. She wished he wouldn't try so hard to hide his concern for Nate.

Kristi cleared the dishes from the table. "I'll need to go get my clothes and explain to Kyle and Francine what happened, if I'm going to stay here."

Jason's eyes followed her movements between the table and sink. His voice was low. "Was there ever any doubt?"

She leaned on the back of her chair, watching him. "I'm going to stay here, Jason, because *I* want to, not because *you* decided I should."

"Oh." He leaned back in his chair, amused at her tone. "Is that the way it is?"

"That's exactly the way it is. When I'm ready to leave, I'll leave."

His eyes darkened to amber as he continued to watch her. "Did you think I had some intention of locking you up?"

She flushed at his tone of voice. "No, I just wanted to make it clear why I'm staying." She hated the amused look on his face and was determined to erase it. "I intend to stay in one of the spare bedrooms." She watched one of his brows arch slightly, but he made no comment as she glared at him.

The silence thickened in the room as they stared at each other. Jason's expression didn't change, although a twinkle danced in his eyes. Finally, he nodded. "Fine with me. Take your pick," He shoved away from the table. "I've got some work to catch up on. Go ahead and take my truck." He paused in the doorway. "You might want to have Kyle and Francine over for dinner, if you're up to it. I know they want to spend as much time with you as they can."

His tone almost dared her to have them over. What was the matter? Didn't he think she could handle the task of cooking for everyone? "Good idea," she responded with a smile.

She heard his quiet chuckle as he crossed the porch and headed for the barn.

Infuriating man!

Kristi crawled into bed with a sigh. It had been a full day since she'd awakened in a sleeping bag with Jason. Dinner had been fun, though. The atmosphere was much more relaxed, as though Kyle and Francine fully approved of her being back with Jason. He'd been his teasing, provocative self, his amusement at her aloof attitude apparent. She didn't care. She was not going to fall into his arms every time he held them open. He was a stubborn, opinionated, arrogant man. Her reason for staying was to prevent Molly from worrying. Jason needn't think she was staying for his sake.

He'd made no comment when she unpacked all her clothes in the front guest room upstairs. When she'd announced that she was going to bed he'd just nodded and continued to read a report Kyle had brought over.

The bed felt marvelous. Kristi couldn't understand why she couldn't fall asleep. She turned over, restless. Then she heard Jason's soft tread on the stairs and knew that she'd been waiting to hear it. She held her breath as he walked past her door and into his room across the hallway. She sighed, reluctant to admit that she thought he might try to coax her into his bed. He knew better.

Kristi was drifting off to sleep when she heard the slight creak of her door opening. Her eyes half opened and she watched the shadow glide silently toward the bed, reach down and lift the covers, then slide in beside her.

"What are you doing in here?" she mumbled.

Jason pulled her against his body, curling around her so she was cupped by his warmth. He whispered in her ear, "Thought I'd find out what it's like to be a commuting husband."

Kristi began to stir.

"Go to sleep, darlin'. Five o'clock's going to come awfully early for you, now that you're back to keeping ranching hours."

She settled into his warmth, drowsily aware of his hand cupping her breast. Then she was asleep.

Six

The spicy scent of masculine cologne teased Kristi as she slept. She stirred. Firm lips touched hers in a soft caress. Her eyes blinked open. The bright gleam of tawny cat eyes filled her vision. She focused on Jason, dressed in a blue chambray work shirt and multiwashed Levi's. He leaned over the bed, watching her indulgently.

"Time to get up, love," he murmured as he continued to drink in her fresh beauty. Rioting curls fell around her face and shoulders, framing her radiant face. She smiled up at him, still influenced by her delicious dream. Lifting her arms languidly she draped them around his neck, then slowly kissed him. They celebrated their being together again with a kiss that began to get out of hand. Jason pulled back, a little breathless.

"Honey, I can't handle that kind of greeting this early in the day and expect to get any work done." He straightened, pulling her from the bed until she stood on the floor beside him. "You've got a busy day ahead of you, yourself."

His hands slid down her slender curves and he jerked them away as though scorched, then backed toward the door. "We'll be in to eat in about half an hour." She watched him grab his hat and heard his heels tapping a rapid retreat downstairs. Stretching lazily, Kristi caught sight of her reflection in the large dresser mirror. Her diaphanous seafoam nightgown hid nothing from view and she grinned, remembering Jason's reaction when he pulled her from bed.

He wants a rancher's wife? Well, he's going to get one, she decided as she grabbed her underthings and walked into the hall. There was a bathroom shared by the upstairs bedrooms and she started toward it, then remembered what Molly had told her. She turned and strolled into Jason's bedroom, instead. It was twice as large as the room they had once shared. She noted that it was more lavishly furnished than the rest of the house and couldn't help wondering why. The plush chocolate-brown carpeting made a dramatic contrast to the blue-and-white of the walls, window coverings, and upholstery. She was surprised to discover that he hadn't insisted on masculine decor for the room. A chaise longue by the window definitely called for a languishing female.

Kristi wandered into the bathroom, took one look and burst out laughing. This was too much. The tub was at least four by eight feet, and one wall was made up entirely of mirrors. Even the shower stall was built for two! All right, Jason, I get your message!

After a quick shower, she dashed back across the hallway, slipped on jeans and a pullover navy blue knit top that clung. She pulled her hair into a rubber band at the top of her head, the long waves falling down her neck and shoulders. It was time to show Jason that she hadn't forgotten any of her skills....

Breakfast was fun. She didn't know any of the new men helping Jason during their spring break from Texas A & M College. Jason's voice had rung with quiet pride when he introduced her to them as his wife. She enjoyed listening to Jason's chuckle during the teasing and talking over breakfast, and she laughed with him when he threw his head back in a hearty bellow at one of the jokes currently crossing the campus.

Was it possible that her presence made such a difference to him? She found herself hoping so. Jason had always been so special in her life—he'd always been there to rely on when she was growing up. She hoped she could learn to give a little of that love and concern back to him. Why couldn't she have understood years ago that it wasn't enough to take his love and support—he needed much the same thing from her.

The hands noisily trooped out to a chorus of compliments on her cooking. Their youthful exuberance made her feel old enough to be their mother. Jason paused beside her and placed his hand on the soft curve of her derriere. Smoothing the curve with his hand, he leaned over and spoke softly in her ear. "We're going to have to fatten you up. A few more meals like that one should do it.''

When she turned from the sink to look at him, his kiss was waiting. The gentle salute affected her as strongly as his most passionate lovemaking. He stepped back and grinned. ''That should hold me until lunch.''

Her first day set the pattern for the several that followed. The news from San Antonio was good: Nate was recovering rapidly. Although the concussion was mild, the break needed traction. It would be several weeks before he and Molly returned home.

The house seemed different to Kristi than it had five years before. With Molly gone, she was in charge. She no longer felt overwhelmed but accepted the challenge and began a campaign of spring cleaning and meal planning with zest.

Jason seemed to find a suspicious number of chores to do in and around the house, so she really didn't have time to miss him before he was there, coming up silently behind her to steal a kiss or tenderly pat a part of her anatomy. No one seeing him could doubt his joy at having Kristi home with him once more.

* * *

The house was finally ready to greet Nate and Molly when they returned. Francine had been helping Kristi with the preparations for their arrival. It was early evening and everyone had gone home. Kristi finished putting everything away in the kitchen and wandered down the hallway to the office where Jason was working. She paused in the doorway, enjoying the sight of him. She glanced past him and absently noted her flower bed touched by the setting sun. She'd planted seedlings of marigolds, zinnias, and pansies, and they were covered with buds, ready to blossom any day. She'd forgotten how much she enjoyed gardening and wondered how she could have been content away from the soil for so long.

Her mind flashed back to her apartment in New York. She had given it surprisingly little thought since she'd gotten so involved here. She rarely spent time in the apartment, other than to sleep. Looking back on her life in New York, she realized how hectic it had been. She'd enjoyed it—how could she not? It had been exciting. Her job had brought her money and fame. She had met many glamorous and renowned people.

She missed Jonathan and his dry wit, as well as several models who'd become friends over the years, but none of them could take the place of Jason in her life.

Jason glanced up from his ledger and saw Kristi standing there, her gaze focused out the window behind him. His eyes roamed over her with possessive pleasure. The snug fit of her jeans reminded him of those she'd worn as a teenager when he'd tried so hard to ignore the voluptuous temptation she presented. She'd definitely filled out since arriving at the ranch. The golden blouse strained at the snaps and he grinned, thinking of her grumbling comments as she dressed that morning. The tips of his fingers tingled at the memory of how much enjoyment he found exploring those curves.

Kristi realized that Jason was looking at her and she wandered into the room and leaned her hip against his desk. She tilted her head and looked at her husband, whose tawny hair was highlighted by the slanting rays from the window. His lazy grin clutched at her heart. She reminded herself that she had come in for a specific reason.

"Who is Alvarez?"

Jason took his time answering as he leaned back in his large leather chair, dropping his pen. He'd been on the phone earlier with Alvarez and wasn't too surprised by her curiosity.

"He's a contact I need in Mexico. Why do you ask?"

"I'm not sure," she admitted slowly. "I guess I want to know why he causes such a reaction in you whenever you talk to him."

Jason's smile faded and he sat up a little straighter. Genuinely puzzled, he asked, "I don't follow you."

Kristi's frown deepened as she searched for words. "Whenever you speak to Alvarez your voice goes icy and aloof—very businesslike. To me it's obvious that you don't like him. But if that's true, why do you talk to him so often?"

Her slightly tilted green eyes searched his, their earnestness triggering a slight alarm within him. *Careful, Jason, here's a test for your new relationship,* he warned himself. *Don't blow it this time.*

Jason stood up and moved over to the corner of the desk where Kristi half leaned, half stood. He ran a callused finger down the softness of her cheek, aware of how vulnerable this one particular human could make him feel. The word *love* was inadequate to describe the tumultuous feelings she stirred within him.

He strolled toward a large leather-covered chair on one side of the stone fireplace, gently tugging Kristi by the hand. When he sat down he pulled her into his lap, cradling her in his arms as though she were a small child.

No one else has the power to reduce me to a quivering mass of sensations, Kristi thought with wry amusement. *I've already forgotten what I asked him.*

For a moment she thought he must have forgotten as well. He began to talk about someone else.

"I've never told you about my friend, Joe, have I?" he asked as he ran his hand along the curls clustered on her neck.

She shook her head.

"Joe Guerrero and I met during Army basic training. He's from El Paso—a couple of years younger than me." He smiled at some thought as he absently stroked the back of her neck. "Joe rushes out to meet life—he's too impatient to wait for it. He's gregarious, exuberant and the best friend a man could possibly want." His hand slipped to her arm.

"Joe and I ended up in the Orient together and were picked for several special missions. It didn't take me long to discover I couldn't have a better man guarding my back than Joe." Jason smiled. "We used to joke about who had saved the other last, but it wasn't a joke—not really." The smile disappeared as memories unrolled in his mind. "You never forget that kind of relationship. Looking back, I realize now it was a miracle neither of us were killed."

Silence lay in the room like a silken net. Kristi could think of nothing to say, and so waited to see what Jason's story had to do with Alvarez.

"Joe returned to the States several months before I did and by the time I returned, I'd lost track of him." Jason paused, as though caught up in a private memory, unrelated to his story. Then his gaze returned to Kristi. "He was one of the men involved in the smuggling investigation. I had no idea he was a part of it until I discovered him working undercover for the Mexican government. Part of Joe's family still lives in Mexico. His cousin got involved with the smugglers and, when he tried to break away from them, they killed him. After that, Joe offered to help the Mexican government stop them." Jason's stroking caused Kristi to want to purr with contentment. "We were careful not to let the drug dealers know that we knew each other, and as far as I know, no connection was ever drawn between us. The arrests made as a result of our work were done when we were 'conveniently' away."

Jason glanced at Kristi and touched his lips lightly to hers.

"Alvarez was one of the men involved in that job. He was supposedly a friend of Joe's, although I doubt that Alvarez understands the meaning of the word." He dropped his head on the back of the chair and sighed. "Anyway, Alvarez contacted me just before you arrived to say that Joe was in trouble down in Mexico and had sent Alvarez to let me know." His eyes studied her from half-closed lids. "Joe is being held prisoner down there, Kristi. I'm going to get him out."

Horrible memories from her early married life came running back to engulf her—nights when Jason was gone, when she didn't know where he was. She forced the word from her stiff lips. "When?"

He pulled her closer, nuzzling her neck. He had to be honest with her. Their relationship had to be based on truth and trust. "As soon as Alvarez can finish making the arrangements. We're hoping he can find a guard in need of a little ready cash. It would make things a lot simpler."

"Why is Joe being held?"

"Joe must have gotten on the wrong side of one of the officials down there. According to Alvarez, some parts of the smuggling operation have started functioning again." He frowned. "Alvarez thinks a minor official wants in on the take and plans to hold Joe as a hostage until he gets what he wants." Jason shook his head. "Mexican jails aren't known for their pleasant accommodations."

"Couldn't he explain he's a United States citizen?"

"Do you think anyone in some sleepy little village cares? Charges were brought against him—trumped-up charges according to Alvarez—and they can keep him indefinitely without ever bringing him to trial."

Kristi could feel the anger building within her. "That's awful!"

Jason felt her body quiver with indignation. "I know. That's why I intend to do something about it."

"But what if bribing a guard doesn't do it?" she asked with suspicion. "What will you do then?"

His tone was nonchalant. "Break him out."

"By force?"

"I certainly hope not, but it may be necessary. Joe and I know a few tricks that might get him out without alerting the entire village. Once I get down there, I'll have a better grasp of the layout."

They sat there in silence as Kristi began to put the bits and pieces of her previous knowledge together with what he'd just told her.

"Was Alvarez the reason you were drinking the first night I was home?"

He looked at her, surprised at the question. "He was supposed to have been there to meet me, which was why I'd ordered a bottle for him." His face expressionless, he commented, "I thought you'd decided that I have a drinking problem."

"I did. You gave an excellent performance of a drunken cowboy looking for a little action that night." Her mocking tone brought a faint trace of red across his high cheekbones. "But you've allowed me to spend too much time with you to buy it." She held up her hand

and started to tick off points on her fingers. "For one thing, you've never had anything stronger than coffee to drink since I've been here, even when Nate had his accident." A mischievous grin flitted across her face. "Of course, the way you like your coffee, that's plenty strong enough." She paused, her eyes skimming his broad shoulders. "Second, I don't think you could stay in such good physical shape and drink as much as I first thought you did."

"Darn, and here I was hoping that you were working at rehabilitating me." He slid her off his lap and stood up.

She looked at him, puzzled. "You *wanted* me to think you had a drinking problem?"

"Not necessarily, but I rather enjoyed your watching over me so nicely." He grinned as he suddenly swung her up in his arms.

"What are you doing? Jason, you idiot, put me down!"

"Huh-uh. I have to maintain my strength and stamina." His chuckle echoed deep in his chest where Kristi's head rested. He took the stairs two at a time.

He pushed the bedroom door open with a booted foot, then shoved it closed with the

same foot once they were inside the room. He
laid her gently on the bed, his hands quickly
unsnapping her shirt, leaving her upper torso
bare to his view. Her jeans were unbuckled,
unsnapped and lowered over her hips in less
than a minute. If there were ever contests for
undressing a woman in the shortest amount of
time, Jason would win a championship award!

Kristi lay there watching him as he jerked off
his boots, quickly discarded the rest of his
clothes and climbed into bed beside her. She
could make no pretense of protest—she loved
this man too much. All she ever seemed to
want to do was hold him in her arms.

He seemed to have other ideas. Kneeling
beside her, Jason started to kiss her, starting at
her ankles and working his way up. She
groaned at the sensations he aroused. She
heard him mutter something.

"What is it, Jase?"

His hands stroked her inner thighs with such
a light touch it felt like a downy feather caressing her. He raised his head and looked at
her.

"Whenever I'm out on the ranch during the
day, all I can think about is you. I fantasize
about all the things I intend to do with you

when I return.'' His head dropped as his tongue drew designs on her inner thigh.

Kristi could feel the desire building within her. As his hands and mouth continued to caress her, her body convulsed in response. ''Oh, Jase!'' His harsh breathing assured her he was not unaffected by what he was doing. She gripped him with both hands, then let go as the sensations of bursting fireworks took over within her. ''Oh . . . God . . . Jase!''

Jason moved his body up over hers as he stretched out between her legs, taking in the dreamy expression on her face. ''Aren't you used to that?'' His voice rasped husky with emotion.

Her voice trembled. ''You should know— you've never done that before.''

She felt his body stiffen, then go very still. She opened her eyes. He was looking at her with infinite tenderness. ''Kristi?'' he said with soft amazement. ''Are you trying to tell me something?''

She blinked. What had she said?

''Haven't your New York lovers worshiped your body as I have?'' Her bewilderment must have shown in her eyes. As he lowered himself so their bodies fit together, he asked, "Hasn't anyone else ever made love to you?"

Caught by the fervent expression on his face, she shook her head. "Of course not, Jase. I thought you knew."

"Oh, Kristi." He sighed as he gathered her to him in a rib-cracking hug. "I didn't want to know—I was determined never to ask—but I couldn't help myself." He leaned down and captured her lips in a kiss so loving that her heart seemed to forget to beat. As he slowly pulled away, he brushed the soft curls clustered around her forehead away from her face. "It wouldn't have mattered, you know, but I'm still glad I've been the only man in your life."

"Jase?"

"Hmm."

"Did you know who I was that night we met in the hotel lounge?" Her eyes were luminous in the soft light touching the room with silver.

"What do you think?"

"I don't know what to think. Are you in the habit of going to bed with women you meet like that?"

"Kristi, I have not made love to another woman since the night you decided to practice your feminine wiles on me and kissed me out by the barn." Gentle amusement laced his words.

"That's a long time, Jason."

"Yes."

"You must really have loved me back then. I wish you'd told me."

"Honey, I thought you knew. Why would I marry you, otherwise? You had me out of my head wanting you, loving you, and I thought you felt the same way."

"I did, Jason.... I still do. I could never love anyone else."

Her comment seemed to cause Jason to lose whatever control he had and he kissed her again with passionate abandon that brought a quick response from her. His provocative position caused her to shift enticingly under him. He reacted predictably by suddenly possessing her with a strong, driving movement. As he filled her she recognized that her body was already sensitive from her previous response to his lovemaking and each thrust caused rippling sensations that made her gasp her pleasure.

His touch drove her to imitate his rhythm, struggling to possess him in the same way. She lost track of everything but Jason and how he made her feel. Eventually he took control, slowing them down to delay their inevitable climax, his hands causing as much pleasure as his mouth and body.

Oh, how she loved this man! His sensitivity to her needs continued to amaze her as he brought her with him to a shuddering conclusion. Kristi was lost in a world of sensation and satisfaction, barely having the strength to grip him to her as they began their long, slow descent.

Jason rolled to his side, taking her with him. Kristi lay in his arms, a peaceful expression on her face. He listened to her soft, even breathing and smiled. Giving her a gentle kiss, he continued to hold her possessively in his arms as he joined her in sleep.

Seven

Molly and Nate's arrival home was a cause for celebration, or so Jason decided after Nate had settled in. He was using a walking cast to help him to get around once more. Jason got on the phone and called everyone he knew for an impromptu party to welcome the couple home.

Kristi stood near the porch railing on the evening of the party, her hand resting on the support post, as she surveyed the crowd of people gathered on the lawn. Everyone he'd called must have come. Kristi saw friends from school—now married and with families.

Multicolored lanterns hung in a large circle, swaying in the soft, warm breeze. A large barbecue pit gave off the delicious aroma of charcoaled fajitas, steaks and ribs. Heaping dishes of salads and vegetables filled the long trestle table set up nearby. No one would go away hungry unless their willpower was stronger than hers.

Laughter drifted from the pit, where several men stood around with beer cans clutched in their fists as they watched Jason turn the meat on a mammoth grill. The signs of strain had disappeared from his face. Molly had commented on the change in him. He seemed more like the young, carefree man she'd watched grow into the responsible, quiet adult. She didn't hide her pleasure at finding that Kristi was once again sharing Jason's bedroom.

Francine hugged Kristi soon after she and Kyle arrived. "Are you sure that's the way a model dresses?" she inquired as she raised one eyebrow. Kristi glanced down at the western-cut, turquoise satin blouse tucked neatly into the small waist of her designer jeans.

Kristi chuckled at Francine's remark. "As a matter of fact, I look more like an Easterner's idea of a Texan than anyone here." They both glanced around, then smiled at each other.

Francine wore a flowing dress that enhanced her petite figure. She nodded. "You're right. None of us would be caught dressed in such a ridiculous outfit." Her eyes danced with mischief as she waited for Kristi's response.

"For some reason, Jason wanted me to dress this way and I'm discovering how much I enjoy dressing to please him." She grinned at her sister-in-law.

Jason's yell caught everyone's attention. "Food's ready, folks. Grab a plate and dig in."

Almost everyone had full plates by the time Kristi appeared at the pit. Jason's eyes lit up when he saw her.

"I wondered what happened to you. Aren't you hungry?"

"Starved. I thought if I waited long enough, maybe you could take time to eat with me." She took in the smile that played across his mouth, a sudden desire to kiss him taking hold.

Jason glanced around, noting what Kristi had already seen—everyone seemed to be busy eating. "I think you're right. Anyone wanting seconds can serve themselves." After heaping two plates with the succulent meat, they helped themselves to the other dishes, found a small clearing under one of the towering oaks and sat down.

When they had eaten most of their food, Jason paused and gave Kristi a sideways glance. "Enjoying yourself?"

Surprised at the question, she responded, "Sure. Didn't you expect me to?"

"I wasn't sure if you'd feel you had much in common with these people anymore." He waved a half-eaten rib in the direction of the crowd around them.

Kristi's voice was scarcely audible when she spoke. "That bothers you, doesn't it, Jase?"

"You're damn right it does. I have no intention of letting you leave me, you know, but it'd be nice to know you're happy here." The half smile didn't cover the serious expression in his eyes.

"Jason, it isn't going to be possible for me to give up my career overnight. I thought you understood that."

Jason's hand paused in midair, holding a beer can halfway to his mouth. With careful deliberation he brought the can down to rest on his knee. "What does that mean?"

"I have commitments in New York that I can't get out of. Things that have been scheduled for months." Her heart sank as she saw his face grow grim.

"Such as?"

"Well, I have to be back in New York by the first of June."

"That's only a few weeks away."

"I know."

Jason took a long drink, then smiled, although the smile never reached his eyes. His voice sounded gruff as he asked, "Do you intend to go ahead with the divorce?"

"No! You knew after the first week that I'd never be able to divorce you."

"Did I, Kristi? You must see me as some kind of mindreader, then. So. We're going to stay married." Jason's gaze took in the milling guests, some of whom were beginning to dance to the taped music coming from the large speakers he had set up on the porch. "I suppose that's a victory of sorts." He pushed himself up. "Looks like we'd better get back to our party. You ready?" He stretched out his hand for her and she placed hers in it, the strength and warmth a comfort after the sudden chill caused by their discussion.

Kristi went into the house and returned with a multilayered chocolate cake and two cherry pies. She set them on one of the picnic tables. Her eyes unconsciously searched for Jason and, when she saw him, her heart seemed to lodge in her throat. She spotted Francine nearby and sauntered over to her, her tone casual. "Who is the woman dancing with Jase?"

"That's Lucinda Reyes. She lives with her brother, Ramon, who bought the old Stoddard place a couple of years ago. They moved up here from Monterey. Probably just got here or Jason would have introduced you." Francine watched her sister-in-law as she studied the couple dancing. "Rumor has it that Luci has been eager to console Jason for his lack of companionship these past few years."

Unfamiliar butterflies lodged themselves in Kristi's midsection. The mutual smiles and warm looks passing between Jason and Lucinda made their friendship obvious, even if the hastily smothered comments around them hadn't given Kristi a clue. What did she expect? Jason was unusually attractive. Just because the locals had always paired them was no reason to expect a new person to understand.

She found it strange that no one had thought to tell her about Lucinda, but from various remarks overheard during the evening, Kristi recognized the curiosity of many of the guests. How would she react to meeting Lucinda?

Lucinda's obvious attraction to Jason was hard to ignore. Kristi had never felt quite so vulnerable as she watched them circle the area designated for dancing, Jason bending close to Lucinda to hear what she was saying. When he threw his head back with unrestrained laughter, a spasm of jealousy shot through Kristi.

They looked so good together. Jason's blondness was accented by Lucinda's olive skin and the midnight hair that fell like an ebony waterfall down her back. Jason's hand came close to encompassing Lucinda's tiny waist and Kristi forced her eyes away from the couple, refusing to punish herself by watching them any longer.

"I don't believe we've met." A low voice at her side caused her to jump. She turned around and saw a slender, dark man with a beautiful white smile. "I'm Ramon Reyes. That's my sister dancing with your husband." His grin was contagious and she found herself returning it ruefully.

"So I've been told." Her eyes drifted back to Jason in time to see him pull Lucinda close against him as he made a swinging turn.

"Don't look so pained, Mrs. McAlister. Lucinda has always known that Jason is in love with his wife." He shrugged, his smile flashing against his dark face. "She understands."

"She cares for him a great deal. It shows."

"Yes. Jason has been a good friend to us both. He has never encouraged her in her feelings." He paused, his dark eyes filled with compassion. "I wanted you to know that."

She could feel the tenseness of her earlier conversation with Jason coming back, along with the beginnings of a headache. "Thank you for telling me. You're very kind."

"And you're very beautiful. Would you like to dance?"

Glancing at the others, Kristi decided to quit lurking in the shadows. "Yes, thank you."

Kristi and Ramon danced, then various other men came to claim Jason's missus. A glass of punch was placed in Kristi's hand and, thirsty from the exertion, she drank it, unaware of the potent additions to the innocuous-looking drink.

Her headache seemed to disappear as she relaxed and drifted to the music. As the last strains of Waylon Jennings's upbeat number about being used, but not used up, died away and a slow number by Willie Nelson began, a strong arm slid around her waist, turning her into a hard, lean body.

She knew the feel of Jason and was already smiling as her head lifted, her green eyes glowing. His clenched jaw barely moved as he muttered, "I believe it's my turn, isn't it?"

She laughed, her earlier fears forgotten. With her head tilted in a provocative pose, she murmured, "Were you waiting for me to ask you to dance?"

He pulled her closer to his body. "Fat chance," he grumbled. They danced as Willie lamented that the last thing he needed the first thing that morning was to have his woman walk out on him. Jason increased the pressure of his arms around her, edging his muscled thigh between hers, causing riotous sensations within her.

"Jason. Behave." She felt her face flush, more with desire than embarrassment, but he needn't know that.

"I'm behaving, love. I've behaved all night. But if these people don't start thinking about going home soon, their host and hostess are going to disappear upstairs."

Her earlier pangs of jealousy seemed ridiculous to her now. She was about to snuggle her head into Jason's shoulder when a movement near the house caught her attention. A slim man who appeared to be in his mid-forties stood just inside the light of the yard. As Kristi watched, he lifted a thin cigar to his mouth, causing it to glow a brilliant red in the shadows. Dressed in black and with dark skin, he was not noticeable to the others.

"Who is that, Jase?"

Jason turned his head, then came to a sudden halt. "Alvarez. Wonder what he's doing here."

As soon as Jason saw him, Alvarez made some sort of signal and stepped back into the shadows. Jason began dancing again.

"What's he doing here?"

"I'm not sure, honey. I'll find out later."

The music ended and several couples headed for the punch bowl. Kristi and Jason followed. Jason had been drinking beer all evening so when he tasted the punch he burst out laughing.

"What's wrong?" Kristi had already drained her cup and was busy refilling it. "Don't you think the punch tastes great?"

"I'm sure it does," he agreed with a wry grin. "Someone's been having some fun— didn't you notice the extra ingredients?"

Feeling a little sheepish, and more than a little dizzy now that she'd quit moving, Kristi shook her head—a big mistake. She put a hand to her face. "I have a feeling that last cup may be the one to do me in."

Jason laughed, his good humor restored as he slipped his arm around her waist once more. "Now I have a good excuse for putting you to bed." He started walking her to the house. Alvarez materialized at his shoulder as he started to climb the steps.

"I need to talk to you as soon as possible." Alvarez's tone was so low that Kristi barely heard him.

Jason nodded. "Let me get my wife upstairs and I'll be back with you."

Neither of them said anything as they went up the stairway. Kristi's headache had suddenly reappeared and she went into the bathroom for some aspirin. Jason followed her to the doorway, concern written across his face. "You all right?"

Without turning her head, she muttered, "As well as can be expected. The only thing to do at this point is to sleep it off, I understand." After carefully swallowing the tablets she managed a grin. "Don't worry about me. I'm going to bed. Sorry I couldn't outwait our guests."

The sound of his warm chuckle wrapped around her heart. "Don't worry about it. I'll probably be up shortly—after I see what news Alvarez has for me."

Only he wasn't.

Surprisingly, Kristi couldn't fall asleep. She had so much to think about. Jason's reaction to her plans to return to New York. Lucinda. Alvarez. She dozed off, her restless sleep filled with bits and pieces of the evening—Lucinda crushed in Jason's arms while he was saying, "I'll never let you go—" Alvarez explaining why Jason had to spend time in a Mexican jail.

She reached for him in her sleep, but Jason wasn't there.

Eight

———

Kristi reluctantly opened her eyes. The aspirin she had taken the night before hadn't helped much, and her head felt swollen twice its normal size. She turned carefully on the pillow and peered at the other side of the bed. Jason's pillow was undisturbed. He hadn't come to bed at all.

The shower helped. She let the warm water pour over her until she felt a little more like facing the day. Why hadn't Jason come to bed? What news had Alvarez brought?

It was almost eleven o'clock by the time Kristi managed to make her way downstairs, where a cheerful Molly exclaimed over the success of the party.

"Too bad Jason had to leave so early this morning. I doubt he managed to get any sleep."

After a reviving mouthful of coffee, Kristi asked, "What do you mean?"

Molly bustled between the stove and table, leaving ham and biscuits in front of Kristi. "He left one of the men in charge—said he'd be away for a few days." She sat down with another cup of coffee and brushed a white fluff of hair from her face.

Kristi frowned, trying to follow the conversation. "He never mentioned anything to me about leaving. Did he say something to you or Nate?"

"Jason quit reporting to us years ago. He must figure he doesn't need to answer to anybody."

Kristi flushed. "He doesn't have to answer to me, either, but it would have been polite if he'd at least told me."

"Maybe he left a note or something."

Remembering how little she had actually seen when she got up, Kristi nodded. "That's a distinct possibility. I'll go up and check right now."

She heard Molly protesting that she hadn't finished eating as she hurried up the stairs and into their bedroom. There, propped up on the dresser, was an envelope with "Kristi" in large letters. *Guess you feel a little foolish now, huh?* she asked herself as she tore open the envelope. The note read:

Kristi,
It looks as though things are falling into place down south. I'll be back as soon as possible. I love you.

Jase

She stared at the note, written in bold, slashing strokes, and realized that this was the first written communication she'd ever received from him. She sank down on the bed, still staring at the paper in her hand. "I love you, Jase." She wondered if she could have that blown up to a gigantic poster.

Her mind wandered back to the young, insecure bride who could have used just this type of encouragement when Jason suddenly disappeared, as it was obvious he'd done again.

Jason had told her that he was no longer involved in government activities. Yet once again he'd taken off on what could be a dangerous assignment. She had a strong hunch that what he planned to do was not legal in any country.

Kristi wandered downstairs to find that Molly had placed her breakfast in the microwave and warmed it for her.

"You were right. He left a note—said he'd be back in a few days." She ate the food without tasting it, thinking of the day stretching ahead of her. She finished her coffee and stood up. "I think I'll see what Francine is doing today."

Kristi made her call and agreed to go over to the Coles'. She needed to get her mind off what Jason was doing—and why he insisted on getting involved in that way of life once more.

Jason was gone for five days. And nights.

The nights were worse. Kristi discovered that no matter how hard she worked during the day, no matter how many hours of physical labor she put in, she couldn't rest peacefully. Either she lay awake or she fell into a nightmare-haunted sleep.

She began to understand how Jason must have felt after she left. It had been different for her. She'd become involved in another way of life. Nothing was similar to her previous lifestyle so she wasn't constantly reminded of him.

Everywhere she turned in this house, she saw him or heard him—and she missed Jason with an ache that left her trembling. Is this how he had felt? If so, how had he coped? And why hadn't he let her know how he felt?

Would she have believed him? She shuddered at the memory of the young girl she'd been, wrapped in her own misery, shut away from anyone's pain but her own.

Life had taught her so much while she was away. She'd learned to appreciate the values that were such a basic part of Jason. The treachery and ruthlessness of the advertising world made Kristi understand how fortunate she had been to have Kyle and Jason, and later Francine, play such important roles in her early life. Their training had given her a sense of self that kept her going during the confusing time when she first became a success. Her love for Jason had kept her innocent of relationships that might have destroyed her.

Although she felt better equipped now to handle a relationship with Jason, she knew she would find it impossible if he chose to continue working for the government or getting involved in their activities. She could only pray that he was sincere when he told her he was through with such involvement.

Kristi went to bed determined to face Jason with her feelings when he returned.

A slight noise downstairs brought her awake and she sat up, listening. She heard nothing more. The room was so dark that she couldn't even see shadows. Kristi slipped out of bed, grabbed her short robe and slid into her slippers. Opening the bedroom door, she peered into the hallway. Soft moonlight from the window at the end of the hall allowed her to see that the corridor was empty. Feeling ridiculous for the heavy pounding of her heart, Kristi tiptoed into the hallway and looked over the rail. A thin slit of pale light came from Jason's office. He was home!

She ran down the stairs, pushing the office door open as she entered. Her breath caught in her throat. He stood there with a torn shirt pulled half off his shoulders, a bloodied bandage wrapped around his upper torso. Her sudden entrance caused him to spin and grab a pistol lying on the desk. She stood there petrified.

"You startled me, Kristi. I thought you'd be asleep." An unshaven Jason stood there, weariness in his voice as he replaced the pistol on the desk.

"What's happened? You're hurt!" She moved toward him, her arm outstretched.

He waved her away. "It isn't as bad as it looks. Just a flesh wound that bled all over the place. I'll get cleaned up in a minute." He looked at the gauzy material of her short robe with lazy approval. "Get back in bed, love—I'll be there before long." He started toward the door.

She waited until he reached her side, then turned and went back upstairs. Jason followed her into their room and stepped over to the boot jack where he pulled off his boots. He peeled off his grimy clothes and left them in a dusty heap.

He didn't look as though he'd eaten since she saw him last. His ribs stood out prominently and there were long creases around his nose and mouth. He started toward the bathroom.

"Were you able to rescue Joe?" Her voice sounded breathless in the quiet of the night.

Jason paused, glancing around at her. "Yes." His face grew even grimmer, if possible. "He's downstairs...we'll talk about it tomorrow." The door closed behind him with a firm click, leaving her standing in the empty room.

She spun around and ran down the stairs once more, going to the first aid supplies kept in the kitchen. After gathering up all she needed, she dashed back upstairs and began to lay them out on the table by the bed.

Jason came out of the bathroom freshly shaven, a towel loosely draped around his hips. Kristi was ready for him. "Lie down, Jason, so I can see what you've done to yourself," she ordered in firm tones. His expression of surprise was almost comical, but Kristi wasn't in a laughing mood. There was more than a slight graze. A jagged wound gaped along his side, looking fierce and angry. Since it was directly below his right arm, she wondered how he'd managed to bandage it.

"Joe knew a family who helped us," he explained in answer to her question. He flinched as she began to place antibiotic ointment along the edges of the wound. Whoever had cleaned it originally had done a good job. There was no sign of infection. He was lucky.

"I take it you put Joe in the downstairs bedroom." She kept her voice low, afraid he'd hear the fear that still held her in its grip, knowing how close he'd come to permanent injury or death.

"Yes. He's in no condition to negotiate the stairs for a while."

"What's wrong with him? Was he shot, too?" She could hear the strain in her voice and hoped he'd ignore it.

"No. He's been locked up for over six months with no exercise and poor food. The conditions were a little tough." He groaned as she began to wind the gauze to hold the new dressing in place. Then he grinned. "You're enjoying being in charge, aren't you?" The tired lines seemed to be easing away as he sprawled on the bed, his towel forgotten.

"Not especially," she grumbled as she tied the bandage. "I suppose you guys enjoyed this little stunt." She began to stroke his chest, glad to have him within touching distance once more.

"It wasn't that bad, actually. Everything went according to plan. I have to admit I'd underestimated Alvarez—he had everything worked out with precision. He works for the Mexican government. Joe was one of his best people. He couldn't afford to leave him in jail. Joe had gotten word to him that he and I had worked out some effective escape techniques years ago. That's why Alvarez needed me. I knew what Joe had in mind." He shifted slightly, then pulled her down to his uninjured side. "Do you think we could continue this discussion in the morning? I haven't slept much since I saw you last." He kissed her on the forehead. "It's good to be home, honey."

Kristi leaned over and clicked off the light. "It's good to have you home, but I haven't forgiven you for leaving without telling me."

He pulled her closer. "I know I took the coward's way out. I discovered that I couldn't tell you goodbye. You and I have done enough of that, love. It was easier to leave a note." He nuzzled her neck and murmured, "You knew I'd be back."

"When, was the question."

"As soon as possible. I don't want to spend any more time away from you than I have to."

His words were softer and slower and Kristi felt his breathing even out into soft sighs. She fell into a peaceful sleep for the first time since he'd gone.

Jason was up, dressed and outside by the time Kristi got to the kitchen the next morning. She looked at the clock. It wasn't quite six and the men didn't come into eat until six-thirty. She had told Molly to keep Nate company this week while she did the cooking. She'd needed something to keep her busy and Molly had understood. Nate wasn't the most patient of convalescents and Molly's presence kept him in better spirits.

Kristi's breakfasts were routine; she mixed biscuits and orange juice and made a large pot of coffee while still thinking about Jason and Joe. She wondered how much he intended to tell her about what had happened. Probably no more than it took to get her to drop the subject.

Kristi heard the men clomping up the steps and across the back porch. As they filed into the room and headed for the table she knew there'd be no conversation until after breakfast. Unfortunately for her peace of mind, Jason started out the door with the men after breakfast.

"Jase?" She stood by the table, fighting to keep her voice calm.

He glanced around with impatience. "Not now, Kristi. I've got to get the men started on some projects that got dropped last week." He pushed open the screen door. "I'll get back to the house as soon as I can." His eyes darted to the hallway, then back. "Try to stay out of mischief, until I get back," he added with a grin. He left, causing Kristi to gnash her teeth in a most unladylike way.

By the time she'd vacuumed the downstairs and put a large roast in the oven, Kristi was ready for another cup of coffee. She'd just poured herself a cup when she heard a noise in the hallway. Glancing up, she saw a man leaning weakly against the doorjamb between the hall and kitchen.

His pitch black hair hung limply across his forehead and around his ears and his clothes looked like something beggars would scorn to wear. They hung on him, making his shrunken body seem even smaller. His olive complexion appeared yellow and only his eyes showed any life. They glowed like black coals set deep in their sockets.

She had to strain to hear him when he spoke. "Where's Jase?" Even the effort of speaking appeared to be too much for him. Kristi realized that he barely had the strength to stand. How had they ever managed to get him this far? Moving quickly toward him, she offered her arm and, in a calm voice, replied, "He's out with the men right now, but should be back soon. Why don't you come have some coffee with me?" While she talked, she guided him over to the table and let him sit down. They were about the same height, but he seemed to be more of a walking skeleton than a grown man. As he rested his face in his hands, Kristi asked in a matter-of-fact tone, "Would you like some breakfast? There are some biscuits left over, and it won't take much to fry some eggs and bacon." She cocked her head and watched him, wondering if he should even be out of bed.

His head came up from his hands and he stared at her as though he didn't understand. Didn't he remember English? She'd forgotten the little bit of Spanish she had learned. Where was Jason, anyway?

When he spoke, she heard only a slight trace of an accent, more of a careful enunciation of words than the slow drawl spoken in Texas. "Breakfast sounds like a dream. Yes, I would like that, very much."

Glad to have something to do so she wouldn't sit and stare at him, Kristi managed to pour another cup of coffee and set it down in front of him, then busied herself once more at the stove.

He had eaten most of what she'd placed on his plate and was sipping his third cup of coffee when Jason arrived.

"Joe! What the hell are you doing out of bed, man? I didn't go to all that trouble to get you back over here just to lose you now." Jason's concern overrode the exasperation in his voice. Kristi heard the warm note of caring.

"Say, amigo, I'm not in that bad a shape. It'll take more than a stinking Mexican jail to put me out for the count." He grin was pitiful, stretching his already taut skin until it looked as though it would split. Kristi noticed that for all his bravado, Joe was shaking so hard he could barely hold the cup.

Without a word, Jason took the cup from Joe's hands, placed it on the table, then scooped him up as though he were a rag doll. He strode down the hall with him and Kristi could hear him all the way.

"Damn it, Joe. You don't have anything to prove to me, you witless wonder. Now, you're going back to bed and this time you're going to stay there. Kristi can make your meals and I can bring them to you for a few days. Just give yourself some time, that's all I'm asking."

She followed them out into the hallway, but hesitated to go into the bedroom. She heard Joe's weak voice. "Kristi? That was Kristi? You never told me she was back, amigo. Afraid I'd try to cut you out, huh?"

The rumble of Jason's laugh echoed down the hall. "You got it. I never could trust you out of my sight. This last little escapade certainly proves that." His voice dropped and Kristi couldn't hear more than a murmur. She started back into the kitchen when Jason called, "Kristi, would you come in here a minute? I want you to meet this character in a proper manner."

She stepped into the bedroom and realized why Jason had chosen it for his friend. With windows on two sides, he could see for miles.

The view was very peaceful and tranquil, and if a Mexican jail had reduced Joe to his present condition, he needed all the peace and tranquility he could find.

Jason held out his hand to Kristi in a natural gesture. As she took his hand, he drew her closer to the bed where Joe lay propped up on several pillows. She noted that Jason had slipped a pajama top on him in place of the tattered shirt he'd worn to the kitchen.

"Kristi, this is Joe Guerrero, a friend who goes back many years." He paused, his eyes sparkling like topaz stones in the sun. "Joe, I want you to meet Kristi."

Joe took in the couple before him with evident satisfaction. "I am very pleased to meet you, Mrs. McAlister. You are even more beautiful than my friend here said you were, which was intentional, I'm sure." He fell back against the pillows. His eyes rolled in disgust. "I don't even have the energy to kiss the bride."

"That's just as well," Jason answered laconically. "In the meantime, the best thing you can do is chow down on her fantastic home-cooked meals and get some meat back on your bones." He strode toward the door, his arm wrapped possessively around Kristi's waist. "Get some rest, now. We'll talk later."

Kristi ran her hand from Jason's waist up to his side. "Should I check your dressing?"

The sun lines around his eyes crinkled as he smiled down at her. "By all means. I'm in need of all kinds of tender, loving care." He turned them up the stairs.

Jason surprised Kristi by taking off his boots before sitting on the side of the bed. She stepped over to him and he pulled her between his muscled thighs. Trying to appear unconcerned, she unsnapped his shirt, only to discover he was offering her the same service.

"What are you doing?" She pulled away from him in surprise.

"Helping you take off your shirt." His face remained expressionless but dancing lights appeared in his eyes.

"I don't need my shirt off to change your dressing."

"I know, but it affords me a distraction while you tend my wounds." His hands smoothed the shirt off her shoulders and lingered on her back. She felt the hook give on her lacy bra.

"Jase!"

"Hmm?" He pulled the scrap of material away and ran his hands along her ribs and upward, cupping her breasts. His touch on her skin set off a quivering inside her.

Kristi tried to ignore him as she removed the gauze holding his dressing in place. His wound was healing nicely, and she quickly placed new pads over it, this time taping them in place.

Jason's hands had been busy while she worked. He had unsnapped her jeans and eased them over the soft curve of her hips so that they fell to the floor. His fingers began an insinuating foray along the lace of her bikini panties, darting underneath to stroke the softness hidden beneath them.

Kristi's breath caught in her throat. She attempted to step back from him only to lose her balance from the hobbling effect of her jeans around her ankles. Jason laughed and pulled her toward him, rolling to his side as he caused her to fall forward onto the bed next to him. "Jason! Your wound," she exclaimed, trying to pull herself up.

Jason's hands continued to be heavily occupied as he slipped her jeans and shoes off, then began exploring once more along her inner thighs. Somewhere in his investigation Kristi forgot to struggle. She wrapped her arms around his neck and kissed him—long, searching kisses to which he responded with eagerness.

Her last scrap of underwear was discarded and Jason's warm hands continued to explore her, causing quickened breathing for both of them. Kristi's hands fumbled at his belt buckle, suddenly urgent to feel his body unclothed against her. Jason seemed unaware of her movements as his mouth slid down her neck and came to rest along the swell of her breast. She tugged on his jeans, but his weight prevented her from removing them. Kristi sat up and yanked at them once more, this time receiving Jason's wholehearted cooperation.

As she pulled his jeans from his long, strong legs, Kristi kissed the exposed portion of his lower body, starting with the inside of his knees and moving upward. She reached up and found his briefs, which she quickly removed. As she continued her explorations she heard Jason's groan.

"C'mere, honey. Let me love you," he muttered as he reached for her. His hand found her breast as her tongue made darting contact with him. She felt him stiffen and he hauled her above him, lifting her astride him. His swollen manhood slipped inside her as she lowered her body over him with a sigh.

Jason pulled her down to him so that his lips touched the soft mound so conveniently presented. His mouth surrounded the peak of her breast and began a pulsing rhythm that matched the strokes of his body. Once again Jason's brand of magic transported Kristi into another plane of existence. Her last coherent thought for long moments was that she loved Jason beyond bearing.

Jason had spent hard days and rough nights away from Kristi, hating the thought of leaving her, even temporarily, hoping she understood the necessity of his sudden disappearance. He had fantasized how it would feel to have her in his arms once again, but none of his fantasies could compare to the reality.

As he held Kristi in his arms while they both calmed down, he knew he would have to continue to fight the compulsion to beg her to stay with him. He loved her too much to force her to stay if she wanted to go but he was very much afraid he wouldn't be strong enough to stand by and let her walk away from him again.

Nine

Although the calendar suggested late spring, summer had arrived in southwest Texas. The days burned their bright way through the morning haze and Kristi began to pamper her flower garden with extra care and water.

Joe also responded to the nurturing he received at the hands of his friends. Kristi soon recognized why Jason enjoyed his friend's company. Outgoing and full of energy, Joe had an indomitable spirit. He kept Kristi entertained with his outrageous stories, most of which were true, according to an amused Jason. Kristi knew she'd miss him once he recovered and continued his travels. She overheard him laughingly point out to Jason that he never held a grudge—he just got even, and Kristi wondered if the person responsible for his recent enforced visit in Mexico might live to regret it. She had a feeling his treks across the border would not cease because of his recent setback.

Jason intended to drive Joe home to El Paso and before he did Kristi invited the Coles for dinner as a farewell celebration. As usual, Kevin and Kari kept everyone laughing with their remarks and antics.

It was Joe who made the casual remark that found its way to Kristi's hidden pain. "I'm surprised you haven't started your family by now, Jase. When we were in the Army, that's all you talked about." He laughed as he finished off his drink, then noticed that the room had fallen silent. He glanced at each face, then back at Jason. "Say, I'm sorry for popping off, my friend. That's none of my business—I know that." Kristi couldn't stand to see him uncomfortable. He was right. Everyone who knew Jason knew how much he longed for a family. Her family needed to understand that she'd come to terms with the past.

"That's all right, Joe. There's no way you would know," Kristi hastened to reassure him. She reached for Jason's hand and squeezed it. "I had some bad luck with a pregnancy a few years ago." Her eyes turned to Jason's and she saw the pain in his. Was he still carrying around the guilt for something over which he had no control? She added casually, "The doctor assures me there's no reason why another pregnancy wouldn't be normal."

Her comment caught everyone as unaware as Joe's had. She caught Kyle's "No kidding?" as she heard Francine's exuberant "That's great news." She waited for Jason's response.

Those tawny eyes glowed as a slow smile crept across his face. "When did he tell you that, Kristi? You never mentioned it."

"That's because he only told me today. I didn't mean to blurt it out in front of everyone." She looked around the room at the pleased expressions. "I'd planned to announce the fact a little later when I had Jason's undivided attention." Her flushed face caused them all to laugh with understanding.

It was much later that night when Jason growled in her ear. "You little tease. You certainly can pick your moments to pass on good news." They lay together in a tangle of sheets, a silent reminder of their earlier activity.

Her smile reflected her complete relaxation and amusement. "At the time, all I wanted to do was to rescue Joe. He looked so unhappy when he realized he'd brought up a touchy subject." She nuzzled her face into his neck, the feel of the corded muscles reminding her of his strength.

Jason's hand slid along her spine, feeling the slight dampness from her recent exertion. He grinned at the memory of her response.

"Kristi, what about your career?"

Her drifting mind came back to earth with a thud. Of course, her career. "Well, I'll just have to call Jonathan and explain that I'm needed here."

"You're certainly needed here, love, but then you always were." His hand cupped her shoulder, turning her so that his lips could find hers. A satisfying silence ensued. "Then you don't intend to go back to New York?"

"I'll have to go back and get Jonathan to release me from my contracts; then I'll have to sublease my apartment and pack my things, but there's no rush about that.'' She snuggled back down into his arms. ''I'm afraid you're stuck with me,'' she murmured in a drowsy tone.

''I'll see if I can take better care of you this time,'' he said, but he doubted that she heard him as she drifted off to sleep.

Kristi was on her way out the door the next morning when the phone rang. Jason and Joe had left early that morning for El Paso; Jason intended to spend the night there and return home the next day. Kristi and Francine had made plans to shop for some refurbishing Kristi had in mind.

She ran back and grabbed the phone. ''H'lo?''

''Kristi?''

Jonathan's voice came as a shock—she had pushed him so completely from her mind.

''Yes, Jonathan. How are you?''

''Damn it, Kristi. I'm fine, now that I've managed to find you. I've been calling all over the Lone Star State trying to track you down.''

''Sorry, Jonathan. Only Texans are entitled to tell tall tales.''

"My, my, aren't we impertinent these days. Your vacation must have done you some good."

"Uh, yes, it has. About that vacation, Jonathan—"

"That's exactly why I'm calling. The schedules have been revised and they're going to be shooting your sequences in the morning. I've been trying to reach you for the past several days. I finally came across your brother's name in my card index." He chuckled. "Couldn't remember your married name."

Kristi appreciated Jonathan's garrulous nature at the moment. She could not have responded to him immediately—she found it hard to catch her breath. When he finally paused, she managed to respond. "Jonathan, there's no way I can be there in the morning."

"There's no way you cannot be here, old girl. It's too late to find a substitute. Besides, you signed the contract several months ago."

"But not for tomorrow."

"Don't be silly. You know the contract states that you're to be available when they're ready to shoot. Well, tomorrow's the day and you'd better damn well be here."

Her brain ceased to function. All she could think about was Jason. What was she going to tell him? Then it hit her. She wouldn't be able to "tell" him anything. He wouldn't be home before tomorrow. She glanced at her watch. She needed to leave within the hour in order to make any connections to get to New York before midnight.

"All right, Jonathan, I'll be there. But you and I are going to have a talk."

"Great. I've missed you. We can catch up on all the news when you get here. Call me back with your flight time and I'll pick you up."

Dispiritedly she muttered, "I'll do that. Goodbye, Jonathan."

Kristi meticulously placed the phone in its cradle as though it were imperative that it be placed exactly. She felt as though all of her carefully made plans were coming apart.

She wandered into the bedroom and looked at her clothes. Most of them would be useless in New York. Gathering her toiletries, she tried to collect her thoughts as well. She'd have to leave a note for Jason, but couldn't even tell him how long she'd be gone. Jonathan was right. The contract guaranteed her availability until the advertising firm was through with scheduled shots as well as any additional retakes needed.

Francine was waiting when Kristi pulled into the driveway. One look at her tear-streaked face and Francine was by her side. "What's happened?"

"Nothing tragic, really. I'm just terribly disappointed. I got word this morning that I have to return to New York two weeks early." She sat down at the table while Francine poured the cure for all ills, a cup of coffee.

"Oh, my. That isn't going to make Jase very happy." She dropped into the chair opposite Kristi.

"I know. What's worse, I don't have time to tell him. I've got to leave now, and he won't be home until tomorrow."

"Now? You mean this minute?" Francine frowned as she glanced at the clock.

"Well, we do have time to finish our coffee, but I'm relying on you to get me to the airport." She paused as she glanced toward the door. "Also, I guess you'll have to get my car back over to the house."

"That's no problem." She was silent for a moment. "Poor Jason."

"How about poor Kristi? I feel every bit as bad about this, you know."

"Except that Jason is going to feel like it's happening to him all over again." She stood up and carried their emptied cups to the drain. "It can't be helped, I suppose. Let me get the kids cleaned up and we'll get you on your way."

Tears filled her eyes as Kristi looked at her practical sister-in-law. "What would I do without you, Francie?"

"Darned if I know. I don't intend to let you find out." They both laughed and Francine went in search of her offspring.

It was after eleven o'clock when Kristi's plane touched down. She felt as though she hadn't slept in days, and her head pounded with every step she took. Even seeing Jonathan's tall, elegantly clad figure waiting for her didn't relieve her depression. The noise bombarded her. She'd forgotten the sounds—the confusion of many voices stridently echoing around her. Had she ever felt comfortable here?

"You're looking marvelous, darling. Such a healthy bloom on your cheeks," Jonathan enthused as he took her overnight bag, the only luggage she had brought with her. "My, you certainly travel light these days," he offered when she explained that there was no checked luggage. "I've got a limo waiting. Nothing but the best for our ice princess, you know." Kristi cringed at the teasing tag. How much of her thinking had changed during these past several weeks? After all these years, why did Jonathan's breezy self-assurance grate?

"I'm surprised I have any color. I've got the grandmother of all headaches," she muttered as she sank back into the luxury of the limousine and sighed.

"We'll get you right home and into bed then. Remember you have to be ready for the all-seeing eye of the camera in the morning."

"Yes, Jonathan. I'm aware of that. Otherwise I wouldn't be here."

"Testy, aren't we? Ah, well, you were never one who liked to travel. I remember the summer we did all those fabulous scenes along the Mediterranean. You actually made the whole trip seem like a chore."

"It was. I felt totally out of place."

"The trouble with you, my love," Jonathan expounded, "is that you're a contradiction. On the outside, you're a beautiful, sophisticated, cosmopolitan woman." He paused, his eyes flashing over the chic golden jumpsuit she wore. "While inside, you're the young girl from Texas who still prefers horses and the wide open spaces to the adulation of the world."

She blinked, then slowly turned her gaze on him. "Of course you're right, Jonathan, but I'd never thought of it." She was amazed at his insight.

"I'm not clairvoyant, Kristi. I helped to manufacture that glossy exterior you exhibit with so much panache. I'm aware how little of it is you."

The rest of the trip was made in silence, as though both of them had their own thoughts to put in order.

Jonathan insisted on going with Kristi into her apartment. Even when she reminded him of the modern security systems in her building, the fact remained, he was quick to admonish, that she'd been away for some time. It didn't hurt to be too careful.

The apartment looked just the same. Even her plants were doing well, thanks to her next-door neighbor. Kristi had forgotten how small the apartment was, she'd grown so used to the sprawling ranch house.

After checking every possible hiding spot for who knew what, Jonathan proclaimed the place safe for occupancy. Kristi managed to get rid of him by solemnly swearing to go directly to bed as soon as he left. She was more than ready.

Her alarm went off too soon the next morning. Her body was still on Texas time. She groaned, knowing that she had no choice but to start her day.

Over lunch—a small salad—Kristi explained to Jonathan why she couldn't stay in New York.

"So what's a few pounds, Kristi? You can take them off in no time." Jonathan waved his hand as though dispersing unwanted weight.

"I don't want to lose pounds, Jonathan. That's my point. I feel much better at this weight. It's probably my normal weight, anyway. I don't want to go around hungry all the time." She looked down at her salad with disgust. Had there been a time when she was content to eat like an underfed rabbit?

"But, my dear, these people call the shots. If they say the camera makes you look too heavy, you have no choice." His earnest expression irritated her. Why did he have to sound so damned reasonable when she felt so contrary?

"All right, I know that, but what I'm trying to say is I don't want to model anymore." There. It was out. She stared at him defiantly.

Jonathan straightened in his chair, his dignity settling about him. In the three-piece pearl gray suit that matched the frosting of silver in his dark hair, he looked every bit the hardheaded businessman he was. "So that's what all this temper tantrum is about, is it?"

"I'm not having a tantrum, Jonathan, and you know it. You've often told me that I'm one of your least temperamental models."

"I must have lied through my teeth, then. Just when did you decide in your wisdom that you don't want to be a model?"

He was taking this every bit as badly as Kristi had imagined he would. She had never attempted to defy him before.

"I'm not sure I ever really wanted to be one, Jonathan."

"I should have known. It was those nasty white slavers who captured you, forced you on the plane, and caused you to seek my help."

His long, slender fingers drummed an irritated tattoo on the table.

"Please don't be sarcastic, Jonathan. It doesn't solve a thing." She glanced around the fashionable restaurant, wishing she'd never brought up the subject. She had to return to the studios in little over an hour. Why had she decided to meet him for lunch and explain why she couldn't stay in New York?

His smile was without humor. "Of course it does, darling. It vents just enough steam to allow me to sit across the table from you and converse in a civilized manner, even though I'd much prefer to jerk you out of that chair and shake some sense into you." He picked up his glass with commendable control and sipped his wine.

"You knew I was married, Jonathan."

"That I did, although I quite distinctly remember your explaining that the marriage was over, done with, forgotten, and it has never been a subject for discussion since. What's changed?"

She could feel the heat burn its way into her cheeks. He was right, of course. She forced her eyes to meet his and cringed at the anger in their onyx depths. "I discovered I'm still in love with Jason."

"How touching."

"Don't!"

"What the hell am I supposed to say, Kristi? I've spent a great deal of time, not to mention enormous sums of money, in building the image that is dazzling every male in this room. Now you tell me you don't want to continue with the career you were so willing—" he stopped, then continued "—even eager to have. What do you want from me?" His hand clenched as he continued to stare at her; a muscle pulsed in his cheek.

His reaction was worse than she'd anticipated. "Perhaps we should discuss this later." Kristi took a large sip from her ice water, the only drink she could allow herself at the moment. She'd had no idea until this morning that she'd managed to gain twelve pounds during the past two months. There'd been a delay in shooting while the wardrobe lady readjusted the waistline of her dress and she'd received a royal lecture on the sins of gaining weight.

"Perhaps we should. I do want to remind you, my dear, that I have been hard at work while you've been playing at home on the range, getting you bookings for the next several months." He leaned toward her, his glance cutting through her like a laser. "Don't you dare try to get out of them, do you hear me?"

In all the years she'd known Jonathan, she'd never seen this side of him—perhaps because he'd never needed to show it to her before. She'd always been biddable, almost passive, in her dealings with him. She never really cared what she did or how hard she worked. Until now. Now she felt she was fighting for her life. She was—her life with Jason.

Jonathan punctiliously escorted her back to the studio, his anger carefully masked as he wished her "good day." A familiar refrain began to run through her mind as the hours passed.

"What am I going to do?"

Ten

The bright headlights from Jason's pickup illuminated the drive as he pulled in. He noticed that the house was dark. Not that he
expected Kristi to wait up for him—he hadn't
given her a time to expect him. He had a feeling she wouldn't stay asleep long once she
knew he'd returned.

He swung the truck in a wide arc and pulled
into the covered shed used for parking. Kristi's
car wasn't in its usual place. He glanced down
at the illuminated dial of his watch—it was
close to midnight.

Puzzled, he crawled out of the truck and headed toward the house. He ran up the stairs and flipped on the hall light. He had made no effort to muffle his steps. They echoed through the house, but he heard no other sound. A sudden fear clutched at him, the kind of irrational emotion felt in nightmares.

The bedroom door stood open and he knew before he turned on the light that he would find no one there. She was gone. He saw the envelope propped up on the dresser, exactly where he'd left one for her, and his mind played back their earlier conversation.

"I haven't forgiven you for leaving without telling me."

"I know I took the coward's way out. I discovered I couldn't tell you goodbye. You and I have done enough of that, love. It was easier to leave a note...."

It was easier to leave a note. It was easier to leave a note. The sentence kept pace with his slow footsteps as he crossed the room. He stood there staring down at the envelope; his name was written across the face in Kristi's dainty handwriting.

He saw images—Kristi when he used to perch her in the saddle in front of him before she'd even learned to walk; Kristi as he sat her in the saddle of her first pony, her pride of possession shining from her bright face; Kristi as she looked the first night after he'd returned home from overseas, her glorious hair gleaming in the light, her eyes warm as she threw herself into his arms; Kristi, lying deathly still and white in the bare hospital room.

"Dear God, I can't go through this again. Kristi!"

His shout echoed through the empty rooms. He picked up her message, then sank down on the edge of the bed. His hands shook so much that he had trouble pulling the single sheet from the envelope, and he flinched as he read the opening endearment.

Jason, my love,

Jonathan called to say my schedule has been revised. I have to be available in the morning.

His eyes sought the top of the page. It was dated the day before. She'd already been gone a day. She was already in New York, back into her other life. His eyes returned to the note.

I hated to leave without seeing you, but
Jonathan reminded me I have no choice—
I signed the contract.

He could no longer read the graceful script
as it began to blur before him. An excruciat-
ing pain filled his chest and doubled him over.

Jason felt that he was in the grips of a chill
as the years without Kristi flashed through his
mind. He managed to strip and crawl under a
hot shower, where he stood and let the water
beat on him while his mind tried to accept the
unacceptable.

Kristi was gone. Whether she wanted to or
not, the fact remained that she had left. The
world of glamour and dazzling lights had a
stronger hold on her than he ever could.

When the water began to cool, Jason turned
off the taps and stepped out of the shower. He
dried himself carefully, then drifted back into
the bedroom. His eyes averted from the bed,
he picked up the note, then walked out of the
room and downstairs. There was no way he
could sleep in that bed. Not tonight, anyway.
He found himself standing in his office, a bottle of bourbon in his hand. He poured a small
amount in a glass. Why not: A little anesthe-
sia never hurt anyone.

He sank into the large leather chair and opened her note once more.

> Darling, I'll be home as soon as I can. I already miss you so much. I'll write every day and call whenever I can. You'll probably be so busy you won't even notice I'm gone.

A groan of pain escaped him.

> (Hopefully you'll discover something missing when you go to bed at night!) Don't ever forget how much I love you.

> Your Kristi

He let his head fall on the back of the chair. It was going to be a long night.

Kristi's schedule had been grueling and she returned to her apartment limp. How had she ever kept up the pace before? She hadn't realized how keyed up she'd been for so many years until she'd completely relaxed at home.

Home. Home is where the heart is, and her heart had been left behind with Jason. As she got ready for bed she called him. The phone rang and rang, but there was no answer. She looked at her watch. It was a little after eight back there—barely dark. If she weren't so sleepy she'd stay up and try to call later, but she was so tired.

Kristi curled up into a ball, clutching her spare pillow in both arms, and dreamed of Jason.

She dreamed she was calling him but he wouldn't answer the phone. It kept ringing and ringing and— She sat up. It was her phone ringing. She fumbled in the dark to find it.

"H'lo?" she murmured, still more than half-asleep.

"Ms. Cole?" a strange male voice asked.

A little more awake, she answered, "Yes?"

"This is Malcolm Metcalf, Ms. Cole. I'm one of the security people here in the building."

"Yes?" responded a puzzled Kristi.

"Uh, I'm sorry to bother you so late, Ms. Cole, but you see, there's a man down here demanding that we let him come up to your apartment." He cleared his throat nervously. "He says he's your husband." His last statement almost sounded like a question.

"Jase?" Kristi rolled out of bed, her tone echoing her astonishment.

"Well, his I.D. says he's Jason McAlister, but he insists he's married to you, Ms. Cole."

Kristi started laughing in shocked amazement. Jason here? In New York?

"I guess it's all right to let him come up, then?" the guard questioned.

"Oh! Oh, yes, of course. Thank you so much. I mean, that will be fine." The phone fell from her numbed fingers as she jumped out of bed. She found the light switch, then reached for her robe. It was the old cotton duster she wore when she cleaned the apartment.

Jason was in New York. He was on his way to see her. She raced to the door and, after shaking fingers unlocked the deadbolts and chains, she threw open the door and stared at the elevator. It remained frustratingly closed. How long did it take to ride the elevator upstairs, anyway? She'd never paid any attention. Now she knew. It took forever.

The elevator doors slid open with silent ease and Jason stepped out. He looked around and saw her standing by the open doorway to her apartment. With angry, catlike strides he advanced on her.

"Jason," she cried as she launched herself into his arms. She almost knocked him over. He paused, but only long enough to scoop her up in his arms. Then he stalked through the doorway, kicking the door closed behind him.

He looked so good to Kristi. He was in a tan, western-cut suit, the style and cut emphasizing his broad shoulders and slim hips. The trousers faithfully molded his muscular thighs and flared below the knee to fall gracefully to highly polished boots. Never had his resemblance to a mountain lion been more noticeable. A very angry mountain lion.

"Why in hell didn't that guard downstairs know you were married? Is it some deep, dark secret you can't share with anyone back East?" he demanded to know.

Jason stood in the middle of her apartment, making it seem even smaller than it was as he glared down at her. At least he tried to glare, but she was too busy kissing him on every exposed part of his neck and face to notice. He stomped over to a stuffed chair and sank into its depths, still holding her. "Answer me, damn it!'' He even roared like a mountain lion.

Kristi pulled back to look at him, her eyes brilliant green in the light filtering from her bedroom, her smile gleaming with delight. ''I'm sorry, I missed the question.'' Before he had a chance to say any more she leaned over and kissed him on the mouth, her lips moving in a soft caressing movement. Her tongue probed his firm lips, seeking entrance. When he started to speak she took advantage of the chance and darted her tongue to meet his. He could no longer ignore her warm touch and the feel of her soft body against him. It was several minutes before they paused, breathless.

''What did you ask, love?'' she murmured as she kissed him along his jawline in front of his ear.

''Why didn't the guard know you're married?''

''Because nobody in New York either knows or cares about anyone else's business, Jase. I don't know the man—he doesn't know me.'' Her hand found the buttons of his shirt and slipped them from the buttonholes. ''What are you doing here?''

"I came to find my wife, that's what I'm doing here." Belligerence punctuated each word.

"Well, cowboy, you done found her. What do you intend to do about it?" she asked, her hands parting his shirt and running over the thick fur of his chest.

"You and I have some talking to do," he stated firmly.

"Talk! If you can hold me in your arms and let me kiss you and rub all over you, and the only thing you can think to do is *talk,* you're older than I thought!" She sat up and attempted to look indignant.

He picked her up once more and strode toward the bedroom light. "You looking for a little action, are you? Well, if you don't want talk, let's try something else!"

Jason paused in the doorway of her bedroom, analyzing the room. He moved closer to the bed and zeroed in on a large picture on Kristi's bedside table. Taken several years ago, it showed him and Kyle laughing into the camera as they leaned against a fence. He vaguely remembered Francine taking it one day, with a joking comment about labeling it "cowboys at work." He was surprised to find it in New York with Kristi.

Placing her on the bed, he leaned over to concentrate all his attention on her. He ran his hand through the fiery waves of hair as they cascaded around her shoulders. She was so beautiful and he loved her so much he ached from it.

She lay there in the soft lamplight, her eyes shining with the joy of his presence when she'd thought him thousands of miles away. Her hand touched the lean smoothness of his cheek, then drifted downward until she felt the roughness of his beginning beard.

"I need a shave."

"Uh-uh. You're just right." Her other hand reached up and cupped his face, slowly pulling him down to her waiting mouth. Their kiss was an expression of their love for each other. It was as though their spirits could only commune through the physical medium of touching. They each found the answer they were seeking—the need for reassurance was past.

"Why are you here?" she whispered as he pulled himself back a few inches, his eyes glowing with love.

He started to answer, and his voice broke. He cleared his throat and tried again. "Because this is where you are, love. I discovered I can't function with a long-distance marriage." He shrugged slightly. "So if you live in New York, I guess I'll be here, too." His voice was husky, as though he found it painful to express the emotions he felt.

"Jason? You can't possibly mean to stay here. You'd go out of your mind cooped up in an apartment in New York City." Kristi struggled to sit up.

His eyes narrowed. "I'll go out of my mind if I stay in Texas, Kristi. I've already tried it your way—I can't go that route again." He took her hand and kissed the palm, gently folding the fingers around it. "I'd rather stay here with you."

"What about the ranch?"

"Nate's almost totally recovered, even if he won't be showing off on any new horses for a while. I'm not worth much back there at the moment, anyway." He gave her a wry smile, "So I might as well learn to like city life." He watched the expressions flit across her face. He could almost follow her thoughts.

"Oh, Jason. I don't know what to say. I can't think of anything more wonderful than to have you here with me, but it would never work. You'd end up hating me." She leaned up on her elbow and gave him a fierce kiss. "I can't deal with that, you know."

"But you were ready to divorce me."

"Yes. I felt the only way I was ever going to find peace of mind was to cut you completely out of my life."

"Which is why you keep a picture of me by your bed, I guess." His eyes danced with amusement.

"But don't you see? That's been the whole problem all along. You aren't just my husband. You're my childhood, my growing up years, my first love, my last love. There was no way to cut you out of my life—you're too much a part of it."

"When did you make that profound discovery?" he asked as he removed the cotton robe and tossed it on a nearby chair.

"When you followed me to my room at the motel."

He slipped the tiny straps of her nightgown from her shoulders. His gaze caught hers in surprise at her words. "That soon?" His tone echoed his astonishment. "I wish I'd known," he muttered.

Their conversation didn't slow his systematic stripping of Kristi, then himself.

"What do you mean?"

"I wish I'd known my plan had worked so quickly."

"What plan?"

"The plan to get you back to Texas." He jerked his boots off, then stood up and quickly pulled off his slacks and shorts, leaving him bare.

"You didn't bring me back to Texas. I returned on my own."

He crawled into bed and pulled her into his arms, making sure each part of her body touched his. "To get me to sign divorce papers."

"Oh, that."

"Yes, that. I figured if I refused to cooperate, sooner or later you'd have to come to me." He grinned when he saw the expression on her face. "That's an old hunter's trick, you know. Stand still and let the intended prey come to you. It took you long enough to fall for it."

"I really thought I could do it, you know," she whispered, "until I saw you that night. I began to have doubts then, but refused to acknowledge them. I even refused to face them when I left you the next morning." She ran her hand lightly across his chest, causing him to quiver. "Oh, Jase, I love you so much." Her kiss promised him her total commitment.

"How long will we have to stay here?" he murmured, refusing to be distracted.

"I don't know. Jonathan is furious with me. Not that I blame him, exactly, after all he's done for me."

"Don't buy into that one, honey. You've done just as much for dear old Jonathan; don't let him kid you."

"He says he's got several commitments lined up through the rest of the year, and he expects me to fulfill them." She pressed her head against his chest. It would never work for Jason to stay here, but she couldn't bear to be without him.

Kristi felt his chest quiver and knew he was as upset as she was. She could see no way out for them. Then his chest shook harder as he began to laugh.

"Jase? There isn't anything funny about what I just said."

"I know, honey, I was just thinking about good ole Jonathan's reaction when you explain to him that you can't possibly fulfill those commitments for him."

Kristi sat up, ignoring her unclothed condition. "But, Jase, that's what I've been trying to tell you. I have to fulfill them. I have no choice." She looked down at him, amazed that he could be so lighthearted. She'd never seen him so relaxed and happy, not for years. Maybe the strain had been too much for him. She began to stroke his brow and croon softly, which caused him to laugh even harder.

"I forgot to mention a message I have for you," he finally said, his grin still very much in evidence. "I, uh, fell asleep in the den the night I found you gone." He winced at the memory of that bleak night. "I overslept. The phone woke me about midmorning." He paused, wondering how to phrase what he had to tell her. "You didn't mention that you'd had some tests run while you were at the doctor's."

Her eyes widened. "They called? What did they say?"

His grin spread. "They said that in a little over six months you're going to have a hell of a time modeling anything but tents, love." He watched the dawning comprehension on her face, glad he was there to enjoy her reaction. With a poor attempt at a frown, he asked, "How come you didn't tell me about having the tests run?"

"I was afraid to tell anyone, afraid I'd imagined the symptoms, and the doctor would tell me I was wrong." She threw her arms around his neck. "We did it. Oh, Jase, we're going to have that family we wanted." Her voice choked to a stop and she buried her head in his neck.

"I know, honey. You can imagine my reaction. It was all I needed to come get you." He pulled her back to him, running his hand down the long length of her spine. "I don't think even your agent can do much about impending motherhood."

"Just let him try," she muttered fiercely. They lay there for several moments, then Kristi leaned back far enough to see Jason's face. "You know, when I first thought about going to Texas I fantasized about getting pregnant, and then having you decide you wanted me as your wife after all." Her eyes sparkled as she met his gaze. "So I guess *my* plan worked as well as yours."

Jason had been patient long enough. His next kiss let her know he was through with light courtin'; he was ready to get on with it. His last coherent thought drifted across his passion-filled mind:

Who exactly had been the hunter?

* * * * *

WESTERN *Lovers*

Coming in November

Two more
Western Lovers
ready to rope and tie your heart!

DESTINY'S CHILD—Ann Major
Once a Cowboy...
Texas cowboy Jeb Jackson laid claim to the
neighboring MacKay ranch, but feisty redhead
Megan MacKay refused to give up her land without
a fight. Surely Jeb could convince the headstrong
woman to come to an agreement—*and* become his
lovely bride!

YESTERDAY'S LIES—Lisa Jackson
Reunited Hearts
Years ago, Trask McFadden had wooed
Tory Wilson—only to put her father behind
bars. Now Trask was back, and Tory vowed she'd
never let him break her heart again—even if that
meant denying the only love she'd ever known....

And available now...

HUNTER'S PREY
by Annette Broadrick

BLUE SAGE
by Anne Stuart

HARLEQUIN®   *Silhouette*®

WL1095-CNM

Take 4 bestselling love stories FREE

Plus get a FREE surprise gift!

Special Limited-time Offer

Mail to Silhouette Reader Service™

3010 Walden Avenue
P.O. Box 1867
Buffalo, N.Y. 14269-1867

YES! Please send me 4 free Silhouette Desire® novels and my free surprise gift. Then send me 6 brand-new novels every month, which I will receive months before they appear in bookstores. Bill me at the low price of $2.66 each plus 25¢ delivery and applicable sales tax, if any.* That's the complete price and a savings of over 10% off the cover prices—quite a bargain! I understand that accepting the books and gift places me under no obligation ever to buy any books. I can always return a shipment and cancel at any time. Even if I never buy another book from Silhouette, the 4 free books and the surprise gift are mine to keep forever.

225 BPA AWPN

Name	(PLEASE PRINT)	
Address	Apt. No.	
City	State	Zip

This offer is limited to one order per household and not valid to present Silhouette Desire® subscribers. *Terms and prices are subject to change without notice. Sales tax applicable in N.Y.

UDES-995

A LETTER FROM THE AUTHOR

Dear Reader,

The story of Kristi and Jason has always been a special favorite of mine. It was the first of several of my novels set in Texas, my home state. I wanted to give the flavor and feel of the area, the sense of family and continuity—and most particularly, I wanted to portray the special kind of man that Texas seems to breed.

This is a story about two people who have always loved each other and yet, have been apart for several years. I could identify with each one of them—feel their pain, understand their sorrow and hope for a resolution to their difficulties.

I sincerely hope that you will, too.

Sincerely,

Annette Broadrick

KK-WL27

Become a Privileged Woman,
You'll be entitled to all these *Free Benefits*. And *Free Gifts*, too.

To thank you for buying our books, we've designed an exclusive FREE program called *PAGES & PRIVILEGES™*. You can enroll with just one Proof of Purchase, and get the kind of luxuries that, until now, you could only read about.

BIG HOTEL DISCOUNTS

A privileged woman stays in the finest hotels. And so can you—at up to 60% off! Imagine standing in a hotel check-in line and watching as the guest in front of you pays $150 for the same room that's only costing you $60. Your *Pages & Privileges* discounts are good at Sheraton, Marriott, Best Western, Hyatt and thousands of other fine hotels all over the U.S., Canada and Europe.

FREE DISCOUNT TRAVEL SERVICE

A privileged woman is always jetting to romantic places. When <u>you</u> fly, just make one phone call for the lowest published airfare at time of booking— <u>or double the difference back!</u>

PLUS—you'll get a $25 voucher to use the first time you book a flight AND <u>5% cash back on every ticket you buy thereafter through the travel service!</u>